French Girl with Mother

A NOVEL

NORMAN OLLESTAD

Counterpoint
Berkeley

Library of Congress Cataloging-in-Publication Data is Available

Cover design by Kelly Winton
Interior design by Tabitha Lahr

ISBN 978-1-61902-784-8

COUNTERPOINT
2560 Ninth Street, Suite 318
Berkeley, CA 94710
www.counterpointpress.com

Printed in the United States of America
Distributed by Publishers Group West

10 9 8 7 6 5 4 3 2 1

For Jenny Ollestad,
my eternal muse

Prologue

I stood on the bank of the Loing River in the French countryside, shivering in my damp jeans, eyes sweeping over the water, my heart thudding. On the far bank, stripped winter trees opened their limbs like refugees waiting to be rescued, giving me hope that it had only been my imagination, a bad dream. A heap of debris broke the surface. I watched it move, circulating in a tributary of current. It rolled and now I saw that it was a body, hunched out of the water, legs dangling behind. I stopped breathing, went stiff and ice-cold. My legs were rooted in place and only my mind churned: the four of us trapped in the château, under the spell of desire, impelled to act dangerously. If only I'd walked away from her that first day in Paris or had left the château before her mother arrived, no one would be dead. What had compelled me to join in her parents' erotic secret and betray her trust? Why hadn't I been able to resist her uncle's illicit offer? It seemed to boil down to one basic impulse that we all shared: we were hell-bent, even destined, to avenge our underlying need to be loved.

one

It all started two months ago. I'd been hanging around Paris for a couple days, waiting to hear from the curator of the prestigious Louver Gallery in Los Angeles. She'd included three of my drawings in a show that opened last week. The portraits were of a Danish woman, Catja, whom I'd met in the Austrian Alps where we were both spending the winter. Catja had made it clear from the get-go that she had a boyfriend back home and intended to return to him at the end of the season. I interpreted her declaration as a warning, as there was always the risk of falling in love when doing portraiture.

The first drawing I made of her captured something pensive and angry in her downcast eyes, a crack in her sheen of milky skin and round face. The crack was my way of expressing something beyond what my eyes saw, allowing me to talk about what I felt stirring in her. Despite her abundantly sunny demeanor, I glimpsed flints of aggression and a darkness she seemed afraid of. I finished the portrait while she stood in the window of a remote hut that we'd hiked up to with our skis. When I showed it to her, her eyes leapt at the image with great anticipation, before she spoke in a quiet, cold voice.

"It's not very pretty . . ."

I'd seen Catja charge down steep couloirs and drink with the best of them at the bars and nightclubs, one of the boys so to speak, and her reaction caught me off guard.

"Do you think it's untrue?" I gestured to the drawing.

She shook her head. Clearly I'd touched something in her that she didn't like, and I quickly rolled up the portrait and poured us a schnapps. As the seconds passed, she grew more and more restless and wouldn't meet my eye. She started packing up her gear and I felt bad for making her uncomfortable. I crossed the hut and gave her a hug.

"It's just a stupid drawing," I told her.

She went limp in my arms but no tears. Will I ever find someone who can take it? Take seeing themselves unmasked? A real partner in crime?

Days later, I tried to draw her again but she would give me only the facade. Nonetheless, I had one strong portrait of her and believed that the other two subsequent drawings would serve as an effective juxtaposition to the gem, really make it shine. I sent them off to the curator and she accepted them for a group show in the fall. With the rejections piling up on me—nine years' worth, nine years of slamming my head against the art world wall—the portraits of Catja had a lot riding on them.

Now it was late September and I was walking along Quai des Tuileries on the Right Bank, the Seine lapping onto the flagstones and the morning sun flitting in and out of the trees above on the boulevard. I'd been scraping by all summer by doing caricature sketches in the streets of whatever town or city I'd wandered into. When I got really desperate for money I'd do replicas of a famous Van Gogh or Picasso, which paid well but which I hated doing because one of the major criticisms against me was that I had no distinct vision. Having to resort to making copies reinforced the indictment.

I'd spent my first two nights in Paris at a hostel in the seedier part of La République, where I'd been drawing the North African immigrants against the sixteenth- and seventeenth-century architecture of that arrondissement's neglected masonry and occasional broken windows. My favorite portrait was of a stately old Tunisian man dressed in a fine suit, which, after a while, revealed itself to be vaguely soiled and threadbare, like the metro sign next to him. Drawing his sorrowful eyes so that they also emanated strength was inspired by memories of my grandfather, who fished the northwest seas off the Oregon coast until the day he died. Grandfather seemed to always know when I needed special attention as a boy, inviting me out to Tillamook to spend a weekend or in the summer a full week with him and Grandma. He would take me fishing, his cure-all, and once, after my pet rabbit died and I was wrecked, he talked about how the sea held all the truth and beauty of life, inescapable emptiness with the very core of sustenance in its depths. The concept was lost on me but its sentiment came through—the enigmatic ocean, like blues music, put things into a certain perspective and soothed the pain.

My phone buzzed. I stopped walking. Cautiously took it out of my pocket. There was an email from the curator, Janet, a Japanese woman whom I'd met at my first show many years ago and who had sadly become my one and only remaining advocate.

Suddenly I was afraid to open the email, paralyzed by a vivid memory from my last show three years ago, which seemed to rush at me with the flow of the river, an arm's length away. Everyone who'd come to the Soho gallery—the collectors, the art enthusiasts, even my mother and father—noticed the *New York Times* art critic entering the gallery. He approached my six pieces, Venice Beach Homeless Portraits, and sighed with tedium, letting his head drop slightly to one side, before stepping away to view the other artists' work in the group show.

The entire room was embarrassed for me and no one would look at me. I refused to slink off and mingled for another hour. The next day, I found out that I was the only artist in the show who didn't sell at least one piece.

Nathan Woods, read the *Times*'s review, *makes pictures for people who want to hang something nice over their designer couches . . .*

My father had come all the way from Portland, Oregon, but only because he'd already scheduled a meeting with one of his New York clients, and he'd brought my mother. At the end of breakfast, before I left for the airport to fly back to Venice Beach where I lived and painted in a small studio apartment, my father put his hand on my shoulder and looked into my eyes.

"Have you had enough?" he said.

I leaned back in the chair, his arm hovered for a moment before lowering, and I glared at him.

"The message seems pretty clear, Nathan," he added.

I nodded and glanced at my mother.

She grimaced, lips folded, eyes unblinking, similar to the look my twin sister Alice had given me when I left the University of Washington to pursue art.

I stood, dropped a twenty on the table, and walked out of the restaurant.

For the entire cab ride to JFK I posed the same question over and over: am I lying to myself? During the flight, every time I shut out my father's condescension and stopped trying to defend myself, grasping a moment of peace, the question would boomerang back in a new form. How do you keep doing it when everyone seems to be telling you to stop? Do you know more than everyone else, is that it? At one point, I noticed other passengers looking at me and I wondered if I was thinking out loud.

In grade school I'd copied Andrew Wyeth paintings and then moved on to Degas and some of the other big boys in high school. That's how I got into CalArts; my technique was as good as the masters.

"But no one seems to want to buy your original work," my father had once pointed out.

I have to keep grinding away, giving it everything I have, living on pasta and peanut butter, until I find my niche, I told myself on the plane. Lucian Freud, a mediocre draftsman who imitated whatever style was in vogue for years, finally found his niche by focusing on painting flesh, cultivating this particular gift to expose the privileged class unhappy in their skin.

The night I got home from New York, I went to visit my neighbor, Wes, an older gentleman who was a writer. He had bad knees and I would take out his trash and water his treasured window box plants, which extended far past each side of the window, too difficult for him to reach. We hung out a lot and showed each other our work and talked about what we were trying to do. He was a very sensitive, gentle man and he seemed to know about everything, which reminded me of my grandfather, whom I couldn't get enough of when I was a boy.

Wes moved up very close to me when I explained how small and insignificant I felt, how downright sad and depressed the whole endeavor of drawing and painting now made me. His glasses magnified his eyes and he peered up at me, searching my face.

"Too much college and not enough life," he told me.

He just blurted it out and I laughed, but he was serious.

Not long after that, he passed away, and I decided to follow his wisdom, buying a one-way ticket to Zurich, thinking the wide-open Alps would somehow help me find my way. Three years later, I was still looking.

A small boat drifted down the Seine into my periphery, ushering me back into the present. A Frenchman with a cane pole fished off the stern while a woman I assumed to be his wife stood at the helm smoking a hand-rolled cigarette. He stared down into the riprap of current. A sculpture of a queen on a rooftop and a big clock hovered above him on the far bank. Paris. The timeless enchanter. Irresistibly romantic. I opened the email.

Hi Nathan,

Many of the collectors had a lot of praise for the Catja Portraits, so I'm so sorry to have to tell you that no one was willing to pull the trigger. If there was one over-riding theme to their hesitation it was something we've discussed before: "No distinct vision. Too inaccessible." (We've talked about infusing more emotion and finding something in the work that is all yours.) Anyway, I'm sure you're disappointed but I still believe in you and I urge you not to give up.

With love,
Janet

I was at the edge of the quai, water splashing onto my Vans, fantasizing about dumping every last one of the drawings and paintings I'd done since graduating CalArts into the river, and tearing up the Catja sketches, all evidence of my fruitless trudge along a misguided path. Senior year, I'd been praised by renowned alumnus Ed Ruscha, who'd attended when it was the Chouinard Art Institute, seemingly ordained to make a name for myself. But now I had to face the reality that I was yet another talent that hadn't panned out.

two

In a haze of confusion I walked back to La République and checked out of the hostel. I wandered through Le Marais with my skis propped on my shoulder and carbon fiber all-terrain ski boots velcroed to a loop on my backpack. Where should I go? Returning to Venice Beach didn't hold much appeal. In other towns and cities, people had been disarmed by the skis and smiled at me as if I were carrying a puppy. Today, the younger Parisians looked right through me, earbuds fueling their strides, reminding me of those times I'd watched buyers step up to one of my drawings or paintings and, unmoved, dart away as if there was nothing there, much like that *New York Times* critic, I realized. That's probably why I didn't mind it now when the older folks barked at me about the skis brushing too close to them, sometimes twisting up their mouths in disgust because they thought I was showing off the good life—it was better than being invisible.

A drop of rain splatted on my forehead. I glanced up. The sun, aglow behind one dark cloud, cast warm hues beyond the isolated shower overhead. As with each failed exhibition in the past, hope began to chirp and pipe. What I really needed was something wild and rampant, I tried to assure myself, something that would jump off the paper and grab the buyers by the throat. But the recycled trill sounded muted now, dissonant, like a broken belfry.

Before giving up on Paris, and perhaps drawing and painting altogether, I ducked into the Musée d'Orsay to study Duran and

Cézanne. The doors hadn't even shut behind me when the concierge approached. He pointed at my skis, glanced down at my wet, tattered Vans, and then moved his finger like a metronome, summarily exiling me.

A message from the universe, I joked to myself.

Minutes later, having to pee badly and not in the mood to be turned away by another Frenchman, I ducked into what I thought was an alley but was just a space between two old buildings that leaned to one side.

In the midst of relieving myself, I heard heels clacking on the cobblestones, echoing from somewhere deep in the corridor, interspersed with the sound of a woman crying. Two figures appeared from what must have been another narrow passageway—a kind of local's shortcut—and turned toward me. Dancing from foot to foot to make haste, I skewed my stream away from them and hoped no one peeked in from the avenue.

"You didn't even come after me," the young woman said in French to the young man beside her.

"But I did. I couldn't find you anywhere."

"It seems that you didn't look hard enough. You were too ashamed of what I wanted to do," she said, and then they noticed me and, thankfully, I was already zipping up my pants.

I faced the sooty stone wall and busied myself with my backpack as they went by.

"Putain," the young woman snapped at me in French. "Are you a fucking dog?"

"Oui. And off leash . . ." I responded in French, my eyes on the young man, not the young woman, all my frustration channeled into the aggressive look I gave him. With my unshaven face and tangled shoulder-length hair, I must've appeared fairly derelict, and as she turned to fire back, he took her by the hand and tugged her onto the avenue.

You're ridiculous, I admonished myself. There's no one to blame, no one to take it out on but yourself. You're peeing in alleyways and have only a few hundred euros to your name because of the choices you've made. Live with it.

three

The raincloud was gone, pushed away by an unseasonably mild wind, when I turned off the quai and crossed onto the Pont des Arts. The bridge's smooth wood planks ran in the same direction as the Seine passing below, and beyond the black mesh railing, I saw the grey tones of the city sprouting from the banks of the river, with the sharp-tipped Île de la Cité dead center, splitting the river in half. The island widened from the pointed end facing me and looked like a big heart with two arteries wrapping around it, feeding the city. An undeniably fine backdrop for portraiture.

Leaning my skis against the railing, I hung my pack from the ski bindings and out of habit unearthed my sketchbook, and my graphite and charcoal pencils, and searched for interesting faces.

There were mostly young lovers on the bridge. Some were attaching yet another lovers' lock to the mesh, already littered to the brim. The routine of clicking closed the lock and the staged kissing and, worst of all, the compulsion to document it with their phones and immediately upload the photos onto various social websites left me numb. Time after time, I'd watched people stare into their phones instead of at the painting on a museum wall, instead of the tree-lined road, a cloudburst sky, that beggar singing opera on the banks of the Arno, or a tortured beauty alone in a café.

Setting aside the pencil and sketchbook, I sat down on a bench, opened a jar of peanut butter, and pasted it on a half-rotten banana with my Swiss Army knife. Maybe it was time to go home and try to get my old job back, answering phones at my father's law firm, so I could save enough money to go back to school. I jabbed the knife into the bench, wiggling it deeper and deeper, as if to kill the idea that I was really, finally, giving up on myself.

Her hand was the first thing I noticed.

four

She was holding a diamond bracelet, tears scudding down her cheek. Instantly, I thought of the girl who'd snapped at me, the stray dog, in the narrow corridor. The guy wasn't with her, so maybe I was wrong. The breeze off the river carried her scent, sandalwood and tobacco and something else—again, making me think it was the same girl.

Hip against the railing, she was impervious to the people milling past her, kissing, posing for photos. She turned her head and looked down at the river. Her fingers were shaking, the bracelet quivering in her hand, the other hand gripping a small leather clutch, and suddenly my pencil was scratching over the paper. Capturing the hand, I moved to her neck, exposed as she craned over the railing. I sketched that detail as quickly as I could. My advantage was line.

You have a natural gift for line, Ruscha had hailed at one of the CalArts exhibits.

Concentrate on the way her head is turned away from the bracelet while her eyes study the diamonds, and the light on the water behind her, diamonds too, and the teardrop on her upper lip, another diamond.

Her eye closest to me arched from the bridge of her nose, fanning wide, then tapered to a feather-tip point. I'd represent them like agave leaves. It happened that fast, suddenly I was lost in an idea, the rush of shapes and color, a puzzle unfolding, and I lived for the spell it put me under. But as my hand guided the pencil, it struck me that I was observing her from a fixed distance, no different from how I'd approached the Catja portraits or any of my work—employing the well-established theory of cool objectivity in order to peer through the subject's mask.

But won't that lead to the same result? You need to try something different or you're never going to break through. This can't go on forever. Imagine spending the rest of your life looking in the rearview mirror at your lost calling.

She folded her torso over the railing. The arm with the bracelet stretched toward the river, and through the mesh and locks I saw her fingers open and the bracelet drop out of sight.

Shit, that looked expensive.

Body still folded, her eyes appeared through an uncluttered patch in the mesh and set on me. We stared at each other. My hand moved involuntarily over the paper, recording her features, suspended upside-down, chopped and splintered by the mesh and locks.

Somehow I needed to get closer, under her skin, comprehend what she was going through and touch the emotional streams, without scaring her away.

She swung herself upright, rocked for a moment, and then came down on her low-heeled ankle-high boots. She looked back over her shoulder at something behind me. I swiveled round—it was my skis.

The girl had put two and two together and now she remembered me, the dog from the alley. She smirked with clear disdain. Black eyelashes sunken halfway over latte-brown eyes. The nose was roman, masculine, handsome; the mouth small, round, with opulent lips, the proverbial tangled bud—all great fodder for a portrait.

But it wasn't enough, not anymore. I needed to mine her depths, not just her surfaces—like Grandfather's sea.

"Am I supposed to be flattered?" she said to me in French.

I put the pencil in my pocket.

"Pardon," I said in French. "It was a good moment and I didn't want to miss it. I'm Nathan."

She didn't offer her name and glanced at the skis again.

"You don't care that someone is in pain?" she responded in English—the classic French slight.

"Of course I do. I was just lost in the moment. I'm sorry."

"But you aren't really sorry."

Her eyes were searing, burning right through me, and it tipped me off-balance.

"No," I said. "You're right. I saw a great opportunity and I went for it."

She'll chastise me and stride away.

Instead she played with her hair, looping a wayward strand over one ear. It was raven black, woven into a French braid. She seemed to be sizing me up. One hand smoothed out her dress, sheer and elegant, falling to just above her knee, fitted yet never hugging any part of her body, and then her eyes roamed across the span of the bridge, impatient, as if I were taking too long to pick up the thread of our conversation. But every response I imagined seemed wrong.

She stepped toward me, a long gait. You'll succumb eventually, her strut implied. Alice, my twin sister, flashed through my mind, and I suspected that, like Alice, the French girl was rarely as confident as her beauty made her appear.

"Can I see it?" She gestured to the sketchpad.

"They're just quick studies."

She came around and looked over my shoulder. Her eyes skimmed the image, she nodded, and I turned the page.

"Do you make a living this way?" she said.

"Not yet."

She nodded toward the pad and I flipped the page, and another.

"You could do well making reproductions."

My eyes snapped up at her. Who was she? An artist? A girl who worked in a gallery?

"It's a great way to make money to support your own work," she explained. "These kind of companies pay well."

I gathered she meant companies that churned out hand-painted replicas of famous works for people who can't afford the real thing—in other words, she saw me as a highly skilled hack.

"That's not what I'm after," I said, and I shut the sketchpad.

She was watching me closely—this man she'd stung with one casual comment—and for a split second her face softened, as if drawn into my torment, and we just looked at each other. The exquisite balance of circles and angles that made up her face, exaggerated enough to have crisp, delineated forms without going overboard, were punctuated by an unruly blaze behind her eyes, an ever-brewing storm.

"Can I take you for a coffee or a glass of wine?" I said. "It's the least I can do."

My voice seemed to startle her, and I guessed she was still in the throes of her fight or breakup with her boyfriend. I almost reached out and took her hand—but reminded myself that I didn't know this person and she didn't know me. That's not how it felt though.

Her teeth scraped over her bottom lip, head moving to one side, the beginning of a shake, and then she glanced at the skis and her eyes lit up, as if transported, making me think the skis had accorded me some sort of novelty.

"Not too far from here there's a good place," was all she said.

I stored the pad and pencils and harnessed the pack. When I grabbed my skis and tilted them onto my shoulder, I gave them a kiss.

five

I finally got her name. Anaïs. She was nineteen. Eleven years my junior. We crossed onto the Left Bank side by side. The way she navigated the streets, flowed and blended with the ancient city, its winding paths, cryptic doorways, and paned windows, blindly running her hand along an iron gate protecting a petit jardin with false chastity, I knew she was a genuine Parisienne. Accordingly, going for a stroll and a drink with a stranger, perhaps a little flirting, was de rigueur, nothing out of the ordinary.

To her credit, she appeared sincerely curious about what I did all winter in the mountains. I explained in French, forcing myself to practice it as I'd done with German, that I mostly lived in huts scattered between St. Anton, Austria—a small ski village where I rented a room in a basement—and Switzerland, sometimes crossing over into Liechtenstein, a tiny country wedged between. I did drawings of whomever I came across and some landscape stuff and would leave my backcountry safe haven and return to the village only when I needed to earn money and restock supplies. I'd either work on the black—illegally teaching tourists how to ski or guiding them around the immediate backcountry—or make caricature sketches on the street.

We were interrupted by a man with round wire-rim glasses and a goatee who began shouting at me about the skis. Anaïs shouted back at him and I noticed the veins in her neck as she rifled off some crude obscenities, making him stand on his toes with offense.

Her message seemed to be: don't fuck with the American, he's with me, and I own this town. It was endearing and undeniably sexy.

"Are we getting close to the café?" I asked after we'd been walking aimlessly for fifteen or twenty minutes.

Her eyes slanted over at me and I felt her palm on the small of my back.

"We don't do things in a straight line," she said as the tips of her fingers slipped under the waistline of my jeans and lingered at the top of my ass. "We like to take the long way."

She studied my face for signs of alarm. I acted indifferent and said, "What happened with that guy I saw you with?"

She shrugged and her hand strayed inside my jeans. "It's the same boys for my entire life. They know how to act the right way and say the right thing. It's like a movie we play a part in. I was trying to shake things up, show him a little truth, you know. But he couldn't bear it."

Moisture percolated in her eyes. She fixed her gaze onto me, something broken, wisps of melancholy, as if she were daring me to stare into it. I tried not to swallow a second time.

"I was showing him a real part of me . . . in bed . . . but he rejected it. Didn't want to see it."

She looked at me with those glassy eyes and I glimpsed the familiar oblivion of rejection, because no matter how big or small the circumstance, it bore its black hole, and my eyes closed for a brief moment, a show of unity.

"Of course he deals with this by going to Cartier and doing the same little dance."

"That bracelet was Cartier?"

"Of course. Part of the script."

"Still, it wasn't cheap."

"Oui." She gave my ass a little squeeze. "He has money so it doesn't mean anything."

Clearly, I was the foil. The new distraction. One without money and far removed from her culture. And I warned myself that I was probably being used.

We came to a street corner and I wasn't sure which direction she wanted to go. Her nails dug into my ass, guiding me toward Boulevard Saint-Germain, and for a brief moment I wondered if she was somehow dangerous.

But it didn't matter. I just wanted to draw her. At least that's what I told myself. Just pursue the repartee a little further and if it turned out to be a total fantasy, so be it. I had nothing left to lose.

"Here we are," she said, lifting her fingers out of my jeans and taking my hand. She led me around the outdoor tables and into the glassed-in part, le milieu, between the inside and the outside sections of Café de Flore.

A waiter rushed across the interior of the café, shooing me away, pointing at the skis. Anaïs cut him off at the threshold, lashing back with two curt sentences, her palm clutching and twisting in my hand. All the men at the nearby tables grinned, while the women scowled.

"Oui, mademoiselle," the waiter said, and he turned on his heel to get the menus.

One of the onlookers, a bird-faced woman sitting next to a handsome man, sighed with disgust and held Anaïs's eye.

"You'll thank me later, madame," Anaïs said without lowering her voice, "when he gives you the best sex you've had in years."

The woman's eyebrows arched, mouth agape, while Anaïs stood her ground. The light coming through the large glass panels separating the sidewalk from le milieu bathed one side of Anaïs's face, leaving the other half in grainy shadow, casting her in a half-moon halo—an angel with a sinful tongue. In the end, the woman lowered her eyes and nodded, and when I turned to sit down, the patrons at the nearby tables were beaming with amusement, as if they'd forgiven her vulgarity because she gave so much life.

I leaned the skis in the corner, hung my pack from the bindings, and sat across from her. She pulled her braid over her shoulder and held it like a rope while she looked at my hands, studying them.

"You seem a bit sad," she said, and she looked up at me, as if she'd read it in my hands.

"I do? I feel really good." I shot her an appreciative look.

"Ah, yes, American optimism. It's even made its way to France."

She frowned and dug a cigarette and a lighter out of her clutch, put the lighter on the table and the cigarette between her lips, and looked at me.

She laughed and handed me the lighter.

"My bad . . ." I said, putting the flame to the tip. "So you're not succumbing to American optimism?" I asked rhetorically.

"Whatever I'm feeling, I'm feeling. I'm not afraid to let it show or to say it." Then her face beamed with a wide grin. "And it makes the smile so much sweeter when it comes, no?"

It was infectious and I was smiling too. She certainly caught your eye, made you wonder, and in concert with the geometry of her face, my gut told me she would explode off the paper.

We drank a good Bordeaux and I sketched her while she told me about her studies. She was a math whiz, working toward a degree in engineering—the only girl in her class. She'd dated two of the boys and even one of her professors. They all turned out to be too weak. Caving in too easily to her. "I need a man," she told me, "like the shepherd in the storm, you know? Who can withstand my violence."

In response, I focused on the structure of her face, transposing it to paper, because if I looked into her eyes instead of at the shape of her eyes, or listened too intently to the thrum of passion in her voice, the way it didn't try to hide the grief while she talked about her father now—always away on business—I would fall like the others fell, and it would all end too quickly. I needed days with her, not hours.

I could feel myself wanting to blurt things out, private fears and vulnerabilities, and I guessed that she provoked this reaction in a lot of people.

As much as you needed to get close, you had to tread lightly. There was no clear line between befriending her for the purpose of the sketches and falling under her spell.

"How long have you been traveling?" she asked me after ordering a second glass of wine, making me worry how much this little tryst was going to cost me.

"Three years," I said, finally putting the sketchpad down.

"Why?"

It was an unexpected question. She seemed to know there was a specific reason I'd left.

"There's only so much failure one can take. The mountains are much kinder."

"Ah, that's the sadness I see in there. You're ashamed of being rejected?"

I nodded. "It's not something I like to advertise."

"So your friends and family don't accept failure as part of life?"

"Not really. But it's not really talked about. You just have to go make it; then you have something to talk about."

She put her hand on top of mine. "This is so different, so totally opposite than how we are."

I looked down at our hands. "I see that . . ."

She slid the sketchbook off the table and began to leaf through it. I had shipped the other books home to Janet and now I wondered what she'd think of Anaïs. The way she touched me and looked into my eyes so freely, even gratuitously, doing and saying whatever came to her, ironic one moment, highly sensitive the next, she seemed to be many things rolled into one—bold and sweet and vicious.

"You're obviously talented," Anaïs said, looking up from the book. "What's the problem?"

"I don't know. Technically I'm sound. The copies I made of Degas, Wyeth, Van Gogh, to name a few, they blew a lot of minds." My voice turned low and deep. "But with my own stuff apparently something's always missing. I just try to get the lines and the mood. A couple simple things. That's all I'm after."

"You want to be classic," she said.

"At least rooted there," I responded.

The second glass of wine came and I lit another cigarette for her. She narrowed her eyes, as if trying to find me through the fumes.

"I have an idea, Nathan."

six

I waited in the café for an hour and figured I'd never see Anaïs again. The stroll, the drink, a little connection, and then on to the next, très Parisienne. The waiter kept passing by, hoping I would leave, but she'd said something to him before departing and he wouldn't dare kick me out. So close yet so far, I lamented. Maybe I could still make something worthwhile from the sketches.

Sitting alone, waiting, was an open invitation for paranoia and self-doubt to join my table. Like any artist, I just needed a little luck. Even John Currin wallowed until he met his muse, an artist herself, whom he eventually married. She'd immediately awakened his desire to embrace the Old Master techniques that he'd been curious about since studying art at Yale, and duly inspired, he started teaching himself painting methods that had been out of fashion for more than a hundred and fifty years. The rest is history.

What about Auguste Rodin and Camille Claudel? I argued. Before it ended badly, she was his model and lover, equally talented, and he introduced her to the scene in Paris; she returned the favor in spades and helped change the course of his work. They fed off of each other. Challenged each other. They took each other to new heights.

Correspondingly, I intuited that Anaïs was that rare uncensored beauty, who had no qualms about letting down her mask, or peeling back mine, and as rash as it sounded, I felt like she possessed, at least potentially, that partner-in-crime element I'd been looking for over the last nine years.

Thirty-five euros was a lot of money for me but I dropped them on the silver tray. *At least you now know she exists; let's hope you can find another Anaïs.* Stepping onto the sidewalk, I balanced my skis on my shoulder, turned left in the direction of the metro, and saw her striding down the sidewalk. I tilted the skis across my face to bury the surge of relief, a heavy groan pouring out. When I lifted them back up, I saw that her hair was now unbraided, a lustrous black flowing over her white cotton shirt open at the neck. The shirt stopped just below her navel, and her low-slung, short-zippered jeans revealed her pelvic bones.

She was walking right into a beam of late-day sun. Her mouth was a splash of pale pink amid the walnut browns of her skin. No makeup, not even on her eyes or lips. *A reminder that her coloring would be as important as her lines. But not as important as getting to know her and trying to understand her,* I reiterated.

"You've changed your mind?" she said, shifting her leather duffle to the other hand.

"No, I thought you'd changed yours."

She grinned, something triumphant in her expression—my impatience, leaving the café like a spurned lover, was concrete evidence that she'd gotten to me, and she clearly enjoyed that.

"Allons-y," she said, walking ahead without looking back, and I followed her.

It was dusk outside the glass ceiling of Gare de Lyon. The train was already rolling and we ran for it, jumping aboard. I'd bought an *International New York Times*, wanting to catch up on the news and prove I had other interests than simply pining over her, and after stowing the backpack and skis, I sat across from her and opened the newspaper. We were on the train to her family's country house.

There was a room for me. A forest. A river. Anaïs would sit for me if I wanted. And the clincher was that her mother would be there—giving me a window into her family life, into things she could easily hide if we were alone, and it would enrich my understanding of her. Imperative if I wanted my work to evolve.

The light changed; we were out of the city, dark green trees and suddenly a provincial chapel framed in the window, then a clearing under a dome of cobalt sky. I peeked over the top of the paper. Anaïs was furiously texting while watching some sort of *Jackass*-type video, giggling and chomping on gum at the same time, and I thought of Andy Warhol's inside joke . . . *everyone will be world-famous for fifteen minutes* . . . and how it had been taken to heart and now had become an epidemic. How could a portrait, made of pencil and paper, with the occasional dabs of color, ever compete with the media shower of infinite and immediate gratification?

She was enthralled with the looping video of a guy riding his bicycle off various second- and third-story rooftops, and her aura dissipated before my eyes. I realized I'd glommed on to the idea that she possessed something timeless, born of classic archetypes, divorced of reality TV and celebrity pop stars, and ironically, by comparison, would reflect something fresh and exciting when I drew her. I lifted up the newspaper to block it out.

I'd created that fixed distance again. Willing my hands to lower the newspaper, I grabbed my pad and pencil and drew her. She chomped on the gum, immersed in the video, and it was disheartening to reproduce it on paper. After a few minutes, she noticed what I was doing and snatched the pad out of my hands.

Her face fell and then her eyes crept up from the sketchpad and found me.

"You're right," she said. "I'm just a boring teenage girl." She tossed the pad back to me. "You still want me to sit for you?"

I nodded, watching her round mouth turn down unnaturally, as she stared out the window, openly affected by what the sketch had revealed. She wore her emotions like an electric wire, so unprotected, and I didn't want her to feel snubbed, so I shared something private.

"A few months ago," I said somberly, "on my thirtieth birthday, I made a self-portrait." She looked over at me cautiously. "After it was done, I saw that I'd made a drawing of an older man with a lot of remorse in his face. It scared the shit out of me."

"Like it was the face of a man whose chance had passed him by?"

"Something like that . . ."

"A man who believes his critics," she said.

"Yes."

"You're only thirty," she asserted.

"I know but . . ."

"Can I see it?"

"I left it in a hut by mistake."

"By mistake?" she challenged.

I shifted in my seat and shook my head. "Probably not . . ."

She watched me, eyebrows raised, letting me know that I'd have to go deeper, open up more if I wanted to impress her.

I wasn't ready, just yet, and stared right back at her. She slid low in her seat and wrapped her legs around my shin, dropped her head back, and grinned.

seven

It was pitch black when we stepped off the train forty-five minutes later. There was no station, only a platform. It was cooler than Paris and there were crickets and lots of stars. Anaïs looked at the sky, lost in thought, and then lit a cigarette.

"Is your mother on her way?"

"My uncle's coming," she said. "I couldn't reach Maman."

Light beams strafed the tops of distant trees then dipped and raked across a rolling field as a car moved along what must have been a dirt road, dust plumes hued red in the taillights.

It was a big Citroën and it skidded to a stop in front of us. Her uncle lumbered out, smoking a cigar, stinking of alcohol. They kissed and then I was introduced to Bernard, her father's older brother.

"Your reputation precedes you," he said, shaking my hand.

I glanced at Anaïs.

"She claims you're as gifted as Beltracchi," Bernard explained with a beguiling grin.

Wolfgang Beltracchi was widely considered a painter of genius and the forger of the century. He'd produced over three hundred paintings in the styles of the great masters and evidently most of them had not been discovered yet, still hanging as authentic works in museums, galleries, and mansions around the world.

"I'll take that as a compliment," I said, garnering as much élan as I could in order to conceal my unease.

"As you should," Bernard said. "She knows her stuff. Besides, Beltracchi is a better painter than 99 percent of the masters he's forged."

"True," I said, "but what makes you one of the crème de la crème is the all-important *idea*, right?" A hard lesson I'd learned over the last nine years.

Uncle Bernard gazed at me before his eyes dropped and one corner of his mouth twisted up in acquiescence.

"D'accord . . ."

When I glanced at Anaïs, she was going around to the passenger's side, moving hastily, partially obscured by the roof of the car, and I was pricked with suspicion, an inkling of an ulterior motive. Then Bernard threw open the door and gestured for me to maneuver the skis between the front seats.

As we came through the first turn, the Citroën bounced to the far side of the road and fishtailed in the soft earth along the edge. Unfazed, Anaïs turned to her drunk uncle and asked him something about his daughter, and he rambled back in very rapid French.

Bernard and Anaïs chatted away as we followed a path beside an eighteenth-century wall, and then he abruptly made a right turn through an opening and onto pavement. There was no indication that he saw the hairpin turn ahead. I clutched the headrest and, as if it were an afterthought, his eyes never leaving Anaïs, Bernard cranked the wheel just in time and we squeezed onto a narrow road, zigging and zagging between battered stone buildings in what appeared to be a deserted village.

I uncoiled when I realized we were driving alongside another wall on a relatively straight road.

"What's the name of that village?"

"Grez-sur-Loing. We just say *Grez*." Anaïs pronounced it *grey*. "It's close to Fontainebleau, which you've probably heard of."

We crested a small hill. Bernard turned and said something I
didn't catch and they both laughed, joking back and forth. In the
light beams, at the bottom of the hill, appeared an enormous wooden
gate that I assumed was the entrance to the country house. At the last
second, inches away, he screeched to a stop, motioned for Anaïs to
stay put, and got out of the car.

She turned around. "You're carsick?"

"No. Just stoked to be alive."

"Ah," she glanced out the windshield at Bernard, "nothing inter-
feres with the French when they want to talk. Especially the man."

Bernard wrestled with the gate. He was a big barrel of a man
whose body was no longer limber. The bottom edge of the gate
caught in the crushed clay, the wood twisted, and he grunted.

"Apparently Maman had to go to Bern today to see Papa," Anaïs
said. "So it's only us."

I tried to dampen my surprise but she saw it in my face and
didn't like it, abruptly turning and sitting back in her seat.

"What does your father do?"

"He works for the French consul in Switzerland," she said as the
gate flew all the way open.

At the end of a long drive stood a four-story château. It took
over the entire horizon, grand and venerable, the likes of which I'd
seen only in photographs, usually in black and white. Lit from below, its grey chunks of stone were wreathed in ivy, cut away around
windows tall enough to stand in. Bernard got back behind the wheel
and we rolled forward. On our left, a single row of vacant stone
horse stables followed the drive. On our right, a weeping willow
vaulted over a lawn, its outer limbs barely visible in the ambient
light, and the lowest branches seemed to be tickling water, presumably the river. As we came to the end of the drive, the river split—the
main body was mostly shrouded in darkness while a channel, made

of hunks of rock with wooden dykes, diverted some of the water beneath the house. Along the château's rutted brick walls closer to the river, I noticed a thin layer of lichen, lime green in the strafing well lights, turning sparser and darker as it climbed higher. The old decrepit château was still teeming with life.

"Nice little country house," I said as we all got out of the car.

"Enchanté," Bernard cheered, shaking my hand, and I realized he was leaving.

"Enchanté."

I watched the Citroën drive away, wondering how in the hell I'd ended up here.

eight

"I always take a swim when I first come back," I heard Anaïs say behind me.

She was standing in a darker area on the grass, slipping out of her boots, one foot on the stone barrier that fended off the river.

"It's become a ritual of mine," she added.

My skis were upright, leaning against my chest, and I wrapped a hand around the tips. With the sound of the river going over a fall and the big château illuminated in the night and the forest all around us, she pulled her shirt over her head and shimmied out of her jeans.

"Aren't you going to come?" she said.

"Sure . . ."

I kicked off my shoes, turned sideways, and stepped out of my pants.

"I already know your ass," she said in a raspy timber, and I looked over at her.

Her hair fell over her breasts and I saw the pulse of that storm in her eyes.

"You think I can't handle seeing your penis?"

I was caught standing there like a shy schoolboy.

"I didn't want to assume anything."

She searched my face before running her eyes down my body and pausing at my cock, as if to confirm that it was filling with blood.

"You're not going to ask for permission to fuck me, are you?" she said.

"But I'm not trying to fuck you."

She started laughing. "I hope not."

Stark-naked, without a hint of self-consciousness, she stood right in front of me and waited for me to say something.

"Can I do a quick sketch before you go in?"

She frowned. "Don't be boring," she said, and stepped onto the barrier. "You missed the best part anyway."

She leapt into the river, disappearing into the black liquid.

It felt like too much of a capitulation to follow her in and I slipped back into my pants. When I turned to find my shoes, her rumpled jeans on the grass caught my eye—a potent detail that I'd overlooked.

I drew the jeans, hard-edged in the artificial light seeping from the château. They looked like those chalk drawings at a crime scene. A splash against the barrier made me turn. Anaïs pulled herself onto the stones and sat with her feet dangling into the river. Black strands of hair clung to her skin like cords of licorice, shedding silver beads down the groove of her spine. She reached behind her and plucked fall-blooming wildflowers from the grass, and the jeans, lying like a body in the foreground, created an ominous effect—the nude girl plucking flowers appeared immune to the dead body or the ghost of one.

I was working fast to capture the moment when she spun around and dropped off the barrier. She picked up her jeans, shirt, and duffle bag, and without a word, walked past me over the footbridge and through the entrance door.

I tried to keep working but without her there it was no use. I gathered up my gear and then wrestled with the heavy entrance door, wedged between the château's bricks, where I noticed a worn, rusted placard that read *Maison Blanchon*, which I assumed was her family name. The stairs to the first floor were off-kilter, cobbled together over decades of repair. Stepping from the landing, I found her in the kitchen.

She was slipping on her shirt. Her damp hair, lying over her breasts, bled through the cotton, clinging to her stiff nipples. I glanced away, taking in the quartzite walls, the modern kitchen appliances, the buckling wood floors, the past and the present side by side. The kitchen was an expanse unto itself, connected to the dining area via an archway.

"Great kitchen," I said.

As if there'd been no awkwardness between us, she took my hand and led me into the dining room. "A little tour . . ." We passed a table that could seat twenty, antique rugs over the wood planks, and an old chest with fine china and silver. Through another archway, she escorted me to the living room. A hearth the size of a VW Beetle, adjacent to which were a small library and a floor-to-ceiling glass door. It opened to a patio, buttressing the lawn, streaked by an outdoor light, where I saw the river bend around it.

Back through the kitchen, we climbed another flight of stairs to the second floor. Two master bedrooms, another small library, and some children's rooms. The third floor accommodated a series of larger bedrooms on the back side of the house, with pitted stone walls and windows framing a view of the channel as it came out from under the château and merged back with the river, dark forest encroaching on both sides.

In one of the rooms, Anaïs pointed to the bed. "This is yours." She stuffed some of the wildflowers in a vase. "I'll meet you in the kitchen," she said, and she walked out.

I heard her pad to the end of the hall; a door creaked and then closed. I put my gear in the corner and sat on the bed.

I was alone with a beautiful young woman in the French countryside. All indications suggested she was an idyllic model, my long-sought partner in crime. Yet I wondered if her aura of confidence and inhibition was just another mask, a game she played to get what she wanted—whatever that might be. A game she probably always won. Was she a gold mine? Or a maze that ends in a cul-de-sac or at a cliff? I didn't know, of course. The only way to find out was to stay on her carousel and see where it led.

nine

She was searching the refrigerator for something to eat when I came down the stairs. With her head buried, she mentioned that her father or uncle would cook when they were here. "Because in France the man does the cooking."

She unearthed several kinds of cheeses and some stale bread. I toasted the bread in the oven to revive it and found a few packets of pasta, a bag of pine nuts, and some olive oil in the pantry.

"With the basil in the fridge," I told her, "I have enough to make a pesto, if you'd like."

"Parfait." She gave me a big smile.

While I prepared the meal—chopping and blending away—she sat on the counter and asked me questions.

"Oregon but I moved to Venice Beach about twelve years ago," I responded to the first one.

"A lot of artists live there, no?"

"Not any more. Too expensive now."

"What happened that made you run away?"

"I didn't run away. I just left."

"Okay," she said, gently. "But something must have happened?" She looked at me with those big pools of compassion and I opened right up.

"In a sense, I had it made, living and painting in a studio apartment, a great old brick building one block from the beach, and I paid

33

for it all by working for a graphic designer. On the other hand, I'd just suffered through another bad show, with a bad review by the *New York Times* to boot."

Anaïs opened her arms, looking down at me with a faint smirk and those sunken eyelids—c'est la vie. I nodded and continued.

"There was an older gentleman named Wes in the building, he was a writer, and we hung out quite a bit. He'd try out his stories on me and I'd show him my drawings and paintings. One day, there were flowers and candles on the sidewalk in front of the apartment building. Taped to the entranceway was a piece of paper with Wes's handwriting on it and someone had written *RIP* next to it. It was the last thing he'd written. He'd jumped off the roof. Died right there on the sidewalk."

Haunted by the recollection, I looked down at the buckled wood.

"It hit me hard," I said with my eyes on the floor. "I couldn't understand. He'd mentioned that his last two books went unpublished but I'd joked that compared to me, only selling a few drawings for next to nothing, at least he'd tasted success. He got up close like he always did when he wanted to make a point. *You start over each time*, he told me. *The struggle is never ending. If it gets easy, then you know you've run out of things to say.* Then he repeated something he'd told me a few weeks before. *Too much college and not enough life.*"

Repeating his words made me smile now.

"I wasn't able to sleep for days," I said, and I stirred the pasta. "I kept turning it over in my head: Wes standing on the edge of the roof, deciding to jump. I kept envisioning him hitting the pavement. It felt, well, soothing. And it stayed with me, that feeling of never being rejected again. And I knew I had to get away."

Perched on the counter, Anaïs made a deep sound that rumbled in her throat, and I looked up. Her cheeks had a scarlet sheen, eyes moist, roaming my face as if buzzing from the experience I'd shared. It was difficult to look at her for more than a second, she was so moved, but maybe I just couldn't bear to see my pain reflected back at me. And it was all mixed up with the anguish I'd felt when my grandfather had died, my favorite person in the world.

Anaïs rocked forward and pressed her lips against my forehead. The sensation spread down my body, joints and sinew plying open, her warmth burrowing in. She combed my hair with her fingertips. I closed my eyes and leaned into her.

"Maybe I can help you," she whispered, kissing the top of my head. "Tell me what you need."

"Just be you. It's already working."

I caressed her long arms, wanted to taste the skin along her neck. But intuition told me to move slowly. The tension, the way we circled each other, probing, felt similar to making quick studies when building toward the fully realized image, and I wanted to take my time finding her. There was also the sneaking suspicion that she might be testing me to see if I would crumble like all the others had. Be careful. There's so much more.

"The pasta is ready," I said.

She ran her palm under my shirt along my shoulder.

"Okay, that's enough, huh?" she said playfully. "Let's eat."

ten

We said good night outside my bedroom and then she walked to her room at the end of the hall, leaving the door ajar. I got under the covers and turned off the lamp and tried to fall asleep.

Her soft caress and the warmth and plumpness of her lips against my scalp were still alive. Naked by the river, she was a great subject whose mystique I just wanted to capture on paper. But alone in the dark now, I craved her touch and felt a shiver of wanting more. You're a game to her. A distraction. Don't forget that. You need to get under her skin but must be careful about how much she gets under yours.

I dreamt of being in Grandfather's boat in a storm, huddled to one side so that it wouldn't capsize from the swells. *When the storm clears,* he said, *the fish will come out, a real bonanza . . .*

I woke up late. Golden light drew me to the window. The autumn forest—oaks, beeches, pines, junipers, growing out of beds of tall grass—produced a mostly green leaf, with the moss-colored river wending through.

I stepped into the hall. Through the open door at the far end, I saw Anaïs's duffle bag. As I got closer, sunlight gently streamed through the windows on all three sides of the large room, washing over the low, empty bed. A good place to work.

I passed through the kitchen, the same as we'd left it last night, down the stairs and out the entrance doorway. Ten paces across the clay drive and onto the small footbridge. It arched over the channel of water that split from the river and went under the château. The bridge delivered me onto a wooden deck that hovered inches above the river. There was a textbook off to the side, and in line with the deck was a submerged levee that ran the width of the river, fifty feet to the far bank. The water bent like a sheet of aluminum over the levee, cascaded for a few feet, and crashed with an incessant gravel-churning noise.

The forest grew over the edges of the river and as I followed it upstream, it looked like a swamp or bayou in some stretches. Farther up, where the river bent sharply, the forest was like a curtain, closing off the water behind it.

Floating on her back, Anaïs came around the curtain. I watched her body drift to within three feet of the levee before she flipped over.

As though she expected me to be standing there, she called, "Bonjour. As-tu fait de beaux rêves?"

"Can't remember them but I'm sure they were good. You?"

A look of ennui was her response.

Water drained off her skin as she lifted herself onto the sun-warmed wood and sprawled, nude, next to my feet.

"I'll be right back," I said.

She was lying on her back, reading her textbook, when I returned with my pad and pencil. Her heels hung just over the edge, almost touching the water, and her black bush stood above her oval stomach, a glossy sheen of ebony amid the ubiquitous sunlight. She didn't groom herself like any of the women I'd ever been with, and I wondered if it was some kind of statement or just a French thing.

I started with the hip flexors, stretching from her lower abdomen, long and defined, emphasizing her undernourished thighs—flat, dull lines. Richer were the two dishes between her pelvic bones and black thicket, and her slender ankles giving way to large feet, and the space beneath her low back, swayed, and the girth of her small breasts held in their width not in their height, juxtaposed to the thick, square nipples.

She looked over her forehead to find me, setting down her book. Her eyes were cinnamon hued in this light, playing off the caramel pigment of her skin. I wished I had some paint, envisioning a plane of syrup browns punctuated by black strands of hair over her cheeks and the black bush coming alive between her legs. Searching for a more extreme angle, I moved to the edge of the deck and lowered my legs into the river.

Drawing her from this low, ground-level perspective accentuated the thriving bush with her torso like a sunken valley until her ripe mouth appeared, and within minutes they became a wonderful paradox to the melancholy I discovered in her face. Her eyelids sank and she rolled her head to one side. She reached that arm up and over her head, shoved her nose into her armpit, and inhaled.

The pencil was down to a nub. My nails were scratching against the paper.

Her other hand appeared, sliding over her thigh and down into the tangle of black hair. I prayed the lead would last. Her fingers curled into the hair, burrowing, and I took down the arm disappearing into the dark void. She inhaled vigorously, sucking up the scent of her armpit, and I sketched that essential image, while waiting for her sex to open up and reveal its color and design. The knees slowly widened. The hand between her legs untangled from the bush. The middle finger prominent.

And then she flipped me off.

Laughing, she rolled over, thighs shut, giggling into the crux of her elbow.

I'd failed to get the hand flipping me off. Seduced by the moment. Yes, I could put the finger in later, but it wouldn't be the same. Regardless, I'd pierced a layer and now I needed a sheltered space where I could further investigate, delve into that battle between what her hand or eye really looked like and what I would impose upon it, informed by our evolving relationship. If the first stages proved to be absorbing, I'd have to convince Anaïs to reenact this moment, perhaps for hours or days, in order to execute the piece.

"Merci beaucoup," I told her as I climbed out of the river. "You're amazing. I'm blown away."

She stopped laughing and leveled her eyes at me.

"Are you hungry?" I said. "I can make us something for lunch."

"Why don't you try to touch me?"

It took me by surprise and I stuttered for a moment. "Is that what you want?"

"How can I know unless you try?"

I kneeled next to her. "This . . . what we're doing . . . feels like an important part of the process. Do you know what I mean?"

She scoffed, jumped to her feet, and walked away.

eleven

When the lunch was ready, I brought a bowl of pasta with large shavings of Parmesan to her room. She was lying across the bed, unclothed, head and shoulders hanging over the edge, two large textbooks and her iPad open on the floor. Setting the food just inside the doorway, I backed out.

"Don't worry," she sniped, her eyes never leaving her books, "I'm not going to attack you."

"I was worried I might attack you."

Her head swung around and her eyes were mean and narrow, while her slightly open mouth seemed to dare me to come and get her. Stay disciplined, I warned myself. Touching her might change everything. Might even make you obsolete. Besides, the second you try to kiss her, she'll probably spurn you.

She shook her head derisively and returned to her books.

"Any chance you would sit for me later?"

"If I'm not too tired," she said. "I'm working on a big school project."

"Okay," I said, and I left.

Before searching for a space in the house to work on the girl-flipping-me-off drawing, I went outside for fresh air. As a rearguard against rushing back upstairs and into her bed, I dove into the river and swam hard against the current.

Anaïs had mentioned swimming to her uncle Bernard's house,

after the bridge and around the long bend. I saw the bridge ahead, a plain concrete structure, and the next time I looked up I was under it. Coming out of the curve, the undertow stronger here, I glimpsed a manicured lawn in my periphery.

Abutting the river, the lawn was a rolling ocean of green stretching for a hundred yards, dotted with bronze and marble statues, until Bernard's château rose up like a tidal wave, twice the size of Anaïs's. She'd told me that the brothers had inherited the châteaus from their parents and I wondered if Bernard got the bigger pad because he was the oldest, or if there was another reason.

The two bronze statues looked like Rodins, and they held me in awe. Their human forms, cutting bold shapes in the air, might be helpful, and I wanted to take a closer look. I pulled my body onto the bank. As I was getting to my feet, a guttural noise raked over the sound of the river.

A black Doberman with a tan patch down its long chest was sprinting from the house. He galloped over the grass, muzzle frothing, chewing at the air. I jumped off the bank, paddling fast, and glanced back to see if the Doberman would follow me in. His fangs flashed and he pranced at the edge of the river. Moving along the bank, shadowing me, he sniffed up my scent, dark wet eyes fixed on me, until I went around the long bend.

I let out a heavy sigh, along with the visions of the dog tearing me to pieces in front of the Rodins, and then turned my attention downriver.

There was a car, an old boxy faded-navy Range Rover parked on the side of the bridge, and a man came out of the car and leaned over the railing, watching me. I went under the bridge. When I came out the other side, I heard someone call my name, and I looked up at the bridge. I saw the man again. He was waving down at me. He wore a straw hat and a high-end field shirt for serious trailblazers that seemed over the top. Instinctively I turned away, as he was too lean and fair to be Anaïs's uncle, Bernard. When I peeked up again, he was turning and walking toward his car.

The current was sweeping me downriver and I wanted to get out and confront the guy. Who the hell are you? But as I went around the sharp bend, I figured he'd probably just mistaken me for someone else, realized it, and left. Or he was speaking French and it only sounded like my name. I mean, no one in the world knew I was here.

twelve

The village market was surprisingly well-stocked, and I bought some arugula and romaine to make a salad, and eggs, cheese, and tomatoes for breakfast. It wasn't easy to part with my dwindling euros but I felt like I had to contribute something.

The butcher was closed between two and three o'clock, so I circled the village. The buildings, sidewalks, and roads were all made of beige- and sand-colored limestone, an Impressionist dream. I heard the purring croak of doves and found them circling a white-stone tower. It must have been from the twelfth or thirteenth century and the white doves disappeared against the white stone and reappeared when they intersected with the blue sky. I crossed to the middle of an arched, cobbled bridge and leaned against the parapet, watching the lazy river. The colors, the silence, the verdant forest slowed everything down, and I thought of the empty château and Anaïs, what potent, conducive ingredients for making art. That didn't mean it was going to be easy. But I'd gotten lucky and I knew it.

In the kitchen, I prepared the marinade for tonight's steak and debated whether or not to go upstairs and see if she'd be willing to work now. No. She's focused on her studies and I have to respect that.

While mixing mustard into the dressing for the salad, I heard her come down the stairs. She appeared, sans bikini top, and when she saw the food on the counter she said, "I'm sorry but I'm eating with Bernard tonight. A business dinner."

"Bummer. Well, I can make steak sandwiches for lunch tomorrow."

"It smells delicious . . ."

She approached me and stood on her toes, kissing one cheek and then the other, her nipples feathering across my chest. She put her hand on my shoulder for balance, fingers smelling faintly pungent, sea salty, and I wondered if she'd been masturbating upstairs on the bed. She pulled back from my cheek, almost nose to nose, her Egyptian eyes resting on me like a curled-up cat.

"You're really a great surprise," she said, and she sauntered toward the entrance stairs.

I pondered the two dimples at the top of her ass and tried to fight back with, "Can we work first thing in the morning?"

"I think so," she said, heading down the stairs, presumably for an afternoon dip.

thirteen

Tossing and turning, I spent most of the night thinking about her, skin toasted brick-brown in the sun, the smell of her sex, and tried to rein in my impulses. With early morning mists rising off the river, I got out of bed and walked down the hall and into her room.

When I sat on the bed, she opened the sheet, as if anticipating my arrival. I slipped under, she turned onto her side and I spooned her, wrapping my arms around her, my hard cock smashed between our bodies.

I kissed her neck, so supple my lips seemed to bleed through to her muscle, and she scooted away.

"Let's work," she told me, "like you said we should."

Pulling the sheet with her, she got out of bed and stared at my body. She stood there, wrapped in that white sheet, and smiled at my desire for her. Was she letting me know what it felt like to be on the other side, the observed model, the one in waiting? Nevertheless, I ached for her and it razed every last thought down to flesh, her flesh. I sat up, slid off the bed, approaching her.

"I better get your materials for you," she quipped, and she strode out of the room.

She wasn't in the mood to pose on the deck where I'd planned to pick up the thread of yesterday's promising image. As a compromise, I drew her in the window. Bed-headed hair, sleep-encrusted eyes, louche against the stone wall, sexy. But I could see now that was just her cover, banal and unoriginal—all she would give me this morning—and I prayed our alchemy hadn't been tainted by my foray into her bed.

Later, while I made omelets on the stove, she sat at the table in her bikini, absent, texting away, and I speculated whether I'd over-reached or had simply given in too easily like the others. I flipped the omelets, watching how engrossed she was with whatever was on her phone. On the one hand she was an open book, I grappled, while on the other, even simultaneously, she remained unpredictable and elusive. How to catch that in a painting?

"Bernard would like to see your work," she said out of the blue, her thumbs punching the keys.

"Well, I have to make something first," I said pointedly.

She cast her eyes at me. "Oui."

"Then let's get to work after breakfast."

"This morning wasn't good?"

"No, it wasn't."

She smiled with recognition, it seemed, for my honesty.

"Is he a collector?" I asked.

"Oui."

I made our plates and brought them to the table. Two chive, chopped-tomato, mozzarella omelets. She tasted hers and made a pleasant noise.

"Are those Rodins on his lawn?"

"One," she said, finally putting her phone down. "The other bronze is a Camille Claudel."

"That's impressive."

"They come and go, depending on business. He's had his ups and downs, but he always finds a way to survive."

"Is there stuff inside the house too?"

46

"Paintings. Most he doesn't own. It's of course a great place to display the work he wishes to sell."

"Right. The kinds of people buying that stuff probably have châteaus too."

She'd already wolfed down the entire omelet and now she said, "Thank you," and stood. "I'll be lying out on the deck."

I finished eating and rinsed the dishes. When I walked over the footbridge, I saw her lying on her side, facing the river. Attempting to focus on the portrait, I glanced at the sketches in my hand as a wave of desire swept me onto the deck. I'd already been burned once this morning for making the wrong move, so I dropped my materials and jumped in the river.

Gravitating to the bottom where it was colder, I clung to the silt until I was shivering, the desire sterilized, and then floated to the top. When I surfaced, the deck was empty, no sign of her. I pulled myself out of the water and was met by the sound of a loud engine, piercing the churning fall. A red Ferrari came to a stop by the entrance door.

fourteen

A young man slid out of the Ferrari. He wore a navy blazer over a white collared shirt, tapered wool pants, and Italian leather shoes—the classic bourgeois Parisian. He had longish wavy brown hair, parted neatly on one side, and I recognized him as the guy Anaïs had been arguing with in the narrow passageway in Paris.

Shit. This could ruin everything.

After he went through the entrance door, I crossed the footbridge and followed him into the house, slowly walking upstairs and into the kitchen, wrapped in a towel.

Anaïs was pulling out a carton of eggs from the fridge and he was behind her, kissing her neck. She flashed me an amused look, clearly enjoying my shock. I wanted to grab him, tear him off of her. The intensity of my feelings startled me and I had to gather myself.

"Henri, meet Nathan," she introduced us, a glint in her eye. "Apparently Henri's decided to pop by unannounced." She set down the egg carton with a sigh. "Famished as well."

Begrudgingly, he shook my hand. I squeezed hard, wondering if he was still her boyfriend or if he'd come to win her back.

"Enchanté."

"Enchanté."

I took over the cooking, wrapped in a towel, bare chested. I wanted to play it cool but after I cracked three eggs into a bowl and began whipping them, I started shooting Anaïs impatient looks. She pretended not to notice and told Henri to come with her to see the new wine cave.

From the kitchen window, I watched them emerge from the closest horse stable, converted into a wine cave, with a bottle of red. Henri was all over her. She wasn't returning his affections but she wasn't pushing him away either. Then she glanced up at the kitchen window and I was leaning over the counter, face inches from the glass. With her eyes on me, I felt something creep up my neck. It was more than jealousy. It was like those locks on the Pont des Arts, bolted down and heavy, a vice clamping around her, and I didn't want to let go. It didn't matter that she was playing us off each other, that I knew she was intentionally provoking me, because she'd forced my hand and called bluff on my last remaining strands of caution. It was a different kind of pull than I'd ever felt before. Grabbing him by the throat and drowning him in the river passed through my mind and I splashed some tap water on my face to cool down. Am I just ticked off that he's screwing up our work routine, threatening to derail me? Or am I getting emotionally attached to her?

They returned to the kitchen and I quickly made his omelet, dropping the plate on the table in front of him. While he ate, they spoke in a rapid wordplay French that I pretended to understand. I did gather that he wanted her to come with him to Arcachon where he had boats and a beautiful house on the peninsula and where their friends were throwing a big party.

I interrupted their conversation. "We need to get back to the portrait before I lose the thread."

I waited for her response, tense.

"Ah, oui," she said, and she turned to Henri. "You're welcome to watch if you'd like. He's quite good."

Henri's presence might complicate the process but I wasn't in a position to dictate the terms. Hopefully he'll decline.

He glanced at his Rolex. "We'll have to leave soon or we'll miss the party."

"Then go without me," she said, getting out of the chair and looking at me. "Where do you want me?"

"I need a big room with lots of light."

She ushered Henri and me to the uppermost story of the château, the fourth floor. At the end of the hall, she led us into an empty space with indirect, soft light filtering from three sides, similar to her room on the third floor but without a bed.

I collected my materials from the deck and some additional materials from my bedroom, and when I got back, Henri was slumped in the corner, brooding, while Anaïs was looking out the window with her back to him. He was already interfering and I thought about asking him to leave, but I didn't want to give him that kind of power.

Kneeling on the hardwood floors, I unspooled the buff wrapping paper I'd picked up at the butcher shop and then laid out the sketches of Anaïs on the deck. Referring to them, I called Anaïs over and asked her to reenact the pose. She took off her bikini, lay on her back, and gave me the finger, crotch a few feet from where I slouched on the floor, and I heard Henri groan petulantly behind me.

Blocking him out, I consulted the sketches, readjusted her, and then got on my stomach for that ground-level perspective. The soft even light of the room as opposed to the slanted shards of sun brought her O-shaped mouth and pubic dome under the same aperture, creating a strange but compelling harmony. It would register unconsciously to the viewer, while enhancing the stiff vertical line of her finger so that we felt its violence in juxtaposition to the fluidity of her body.

As if sinking to the bottom of the ocean, all the turbulence of the day was obliterated by the exertion of drawing. It was the first time I'd ever worked down on the floor like Pollock, and I was deep in the throes, when Henri suddenly stepped onto the paper, inches from my hand.

"That's not her," he said, his royal blue eyes brimming with condescension. "Too barbaric."

"Well, that's what I see."

"It's time to go," he barked at Anaïs, still sprawled on the floor.

She looked up at him and then over at me, tilting her head as if to ask, What do you have to say about that?

Again, I wondered how they'd left it in Paris. The diamond bracelet dropped in the river.

"Do you want to go with him?" I asked her.

"It's none of your business," Henri protested.

"I'm not talking to you."

"If I go away for a few days," she said, "will you wait for me?"

She was completely nude, exposed physically and emotionally to the two men vying for her attention. While it was a kind of weapon she wielded, I also appreciated her aplomb.

"Yes," I said, wanting to accept her challenge, and because, most critically, I feared saying no might jeopardize any chance of working with her again.

Her face washed into ovals and spheres, the angles rounded, and her eyes rested on me while she got to her feet.

Henri stepped between us, handing over her bikini.

She didn't put it on. "I'll be back in a couple days, Nathan," she said, glancing at me over her shoulder, walking out the door.

fifteen

Right away, it felt lonely in the big château and I wondered how I would get through it. I went to bed early, awoke at dawn, and got to work. By noon, I had talked myself into the idea that the image of her flipping me off was strong and would make for a good painting. I wanted to get a canvas and paints and experiment with color. It had been too long since I'd worked with anything but pencil, and now I heard the critics in my head: you cannot do it—paint, color, an entire undeveloped part of your work that will be your undoing.

I went outside and jumped in the river. I needed to calm down before I returned to the drawing. At the concrete bridge, winded, I rested at its base on a rock footing, wondering where I'd go if she didn't come back. The Alps, once my safe haven, seemed bleak and cold.

Clambering echoed along the underside of the bridge, and then that man with the straw hat and pale face came trotting down the far-side embankment. I stayed very still, shadowed under the bridge, as he walked upstream along the bank, a pair of binoculars around his neck and a book in one hand. As he went around the long bend, I saw him lift the binoculars to his eyes.

Propelling into the headwind of current, I eased around the bend. When I spotted him, mixed in among the first row of trees, I let the current sweep me against the bank on his side, where it eclipsed me from view. I caught my breath and peeked over the bank. The binoculars were pressed to the man's face, pointed across the river, and on the cover of the book in his hand, I made out pictures of birds.

I lowered and turned. Directly across the water was Bernard's lawn. On its far side, abutting the château, Bernard was sitting on the patio, having a drink and a cigar with a swarthy-looking man in a designer suit.

The Doberman stood up. He must have been lying at Bernard's feet. His ears were spiked, alert, and his snout was aimed at the river.

I heard the man's footfalls crunching dead leaves and when I peeked again he'd trailed away into the interior of the forest. I let the current drag me away.

It was a little odd but it actually made sense, I concluded, drifting. The guy was out bird-watching and couldn't resist taking a gander at that amazing château with the statues on the lawn. Who wouldn't be curious? Thinking of the Claudel sparked the urge to hear Anaïs's voice, but I didn't have her number.

After pilfering a couple reds from the wine cave, I drifted around the creaky halls and vacant rooms, stumbling upon a book in English on the shelf in the library. The words warbled, making me nauseous, and I put it back.

Later, still unable to sleep, I returned to the kitchen and made a hamburger from ground sirloin, the familiarity meant to soothe me. It only sobered me up and brought the emptiness a little closer.

What she's asking of me—to wait for her while she spends time with another man, likely fucking him—verges on humiliation. Who cares? I reproached. You need to stay focused on the work, without allowing the simmering desire to get in the way. Maybe I should leave my number and find a hostel, let her call me when she gets back? Exhibit a little self-respect. My phone card had run out of minutes so I'd have to get a new one, and then thinking of paying for the hostel, really burning through my dwindling euros, closed the door on that option.

Another day and night passed and on the fourth night, I woke up filled with dread. It felt like a hatch opening inside my chest, revealing a remote chamber, packed with my greatest regrets: a litany of men and women shaking their heads, turning away, shunning my work.

Not feeling it . . .
Doesn't quite achieve . . .
Misses . . .
Are any of his reproductions from art school available?

I rolled over and looked at the ceiling. What happens if she doesn't come back?

sixteen

In the morning, I wandered down to the kitchen to force myself to eat and to figure out where I'd go. Anaïs was making coffee. She scowled at me and I leaned against the railing, stewing with resentment for what I'd allowed her to put me through. She wore a new short sheer dress and her hair was up, eyes tired, creased, as if she'd had a long night. We watched each other for a moment. I hadn't noticed the Ferrari out the window but that didn't mean anything.

"Why did you let me go?" she said with an accusatory edge that was outlandish under the circumstances.

"I trusted you'd come back," I said cavalierly.

"A French man would have never let me go. Not without a fight."

I nodded. Keeping a lid on my emotions.

"I liked that you didn't try to possess me, but then it made me angry."

"You wanted it both ways, huh?"

"Of course."

Her mouth was soft, pliant, eyes drowsy, the antithesis of defensive—this is me. But I wasn't going to succumb, and I glanced away.

"You're pissed off?"

I shrugged.

"Did you want to fight or was it easy to let me go?" she asked.

"I almost grabbed him by the fucking neck and threw him in the river, but," I fixed my eyes on her with indignation, "I thought it would be better to just let you come back on your own."

"So you were jealous?"

I tried to withhold the answer but eventually nodded.

"It hurt you?"

I paused. "Yes."

She stepped forward, raked her fingers up the back of my scalp, nails scratching the skin, and kissed me. Her tongue swirled, indulgent and slow, and she pressed herself against my chest.

"You're a sweet man, Nathan . . ." Her voice surprisingly soft and yielding, and it swished between my temples and my head lightened. The turbulence coming off her skin, its voltage, was disorienting, like the onset of a fever, and my lips were dry, thirsty, in need of water. It was hot, everything lanced in heat.

When my eyes came into focus, I was kissing my way down her spine, her palms on the edge of the counter, and I ripped the dress off her shoulder. The crack of her ass was a shade darker, oaken, and following its groove, I grazed my tongue tip along her goose bumps. She drew in air, a sizzling hiss, and I nestled my face between her thighs.

Within seconds, she was easing down to the floor and she rested onto her back. I never lost contact, gently teasing and licking and tasting her. She spoke in French. She shuddered. Growled low. Then silence. Perhaps she'd lost her nerve or the vein of her excitement. In reaction, I circled very slowly and hoped she'd find her way back.

The first quiver arrived in her hand clutching my head. The thighs shook. Her belly caved and she called out, "Non, non, non."

I carried her in my arms and laid her down on the antique couch beside the big hearth. She stretched out on the velvet. I kissed her neck and ears and mouth and she reached down and guided me inside her. She held on to my back and pressed her torso and thighs tight to my skin. She whispered in my ear and we were tender until the moment of climax.

"Promise you'll always be hungry for me," she said.

"I promise."

"Nail me to the ground."

I gathered up her black mane and tugged hard for leverage.

seventeen

We drove Bernard's Citroën to Fontainebleau and bought my materials: gouache greens, blues, greys, browns, and pinks, and big sheets of high-quality paper.

She sat for me for five consecutive days, moving between the deck and the fourth-floor room on the end with views of the river and smooth light, reenacting that moment when she'd flipped me off. The gouache paint was applied in deliberately clumsy stains and dabs, bleeding over the graphite lines and charcoal shadings. We had to go back to Fontainebleau to buy black gouache for her hair and bush, as the blues nudged the image too far into an ideal.

We swam every morning and ate sporadically as if sex and painting would sustain us, and at night we talked about where we would go once the drawings were done.

When the first portrait was nearly finished, Anaïs clipped the top edge of it to a wire I'd hung with duct tape along the back wall in the fourth-floor room. In a kind of stream of consciousness, she paced back and forth, dissecting the work.

"I like how you allow us to feel the bones through the flesh. It evokes deep, hidden emotions."

Now I recognized the skeletal presence in her form and thought that I'd never done it to that extreme before. Some new idea emerging.

"And you must admire Egon Schiele."

"Yes, for sure."

"Your use of gouache," she said, leaning in close to the drawing, studying the subtle dabs of red around the stiff fuck-you finger, "just sort of accenting with it and not feeling the need to make the colors true to life, c'est très Schiele."

I saw it now and nodded.

"And you could learn from the way he embraces everything you seem to shy away from, the various forms of desire."

I glanced at her, tilted my head. "Oh, yeah?"

"Desire is full of violence and pain, even fear."

"Well," I quipped, "ever since I met you, I've been acutely in touch with those things."

"Oui," she said with utter nonchalance. "Don't you see how your work has changed?" She gestured at my pile of materials, specifically at the worn drawing pad opened to the old Tunisian man in the threadbare suit. She squatted and slid it beside the portrait of her.

Probing the two portraits through the lens of her observations, I saw the jagged, irrational shapes in her image, as opposed to the correct, meticulous lines of the old man.

"I don't mean to take the credit," she said.

"No. You really bring what is stuck below to the surface," I told her. "You let it shine out of you, what most people keep hidden, and it makes for great images."

"It's not me that you're seeing, Nathan. It's you."

I turned and studied her portrait again. My eye fell first on her forlorn expression, a lost soul, then the puff of her lips, bold, contradicting the rest of her face, and seemingly below it all was her pubic dome where life began, in sheer counterpoint to the stiff fuck-you finger.

Her image, perhaps its dual spheres, brought me back to the ocean, off the coast of Oregon, to my childhood.

"In a way, it reminds me of the ocean," I said, glancing between the portrait and her. "Whenever I went out fishing with Grandfather, he would talk about the wind and the sea and the life below, how it contained its own moods and even feelings, like people. *The difference is*, he said, *nature follows certain laws, while human nature is messy and doesn't follow any laws."*

Anaïs's shoulders drew back and her head turned in a small arc, eyes on me, a gesture of appreciation, beckoning me to tell her more.

"He was so stoic on land. Barely said a word. But out at sea he talked about all kinds of things. I think he sort of whet my curiosity about the contradictions and paradoxes in us," I continued. "I remember fishing on a really choppy day, and I asked him why Grandma never came out. *She hates boats and the smell of fish,* he told me. He must've seen the startled look on my face, as he made his living fishing and always smelled of fish. *But we enjoy each other's sense of humor and I love her music and I think she likes my wild stories about the sea,"* he explained. *We give each other what the other is missing."*

My voice changed. "He died when I was twelve."

Anaïs reached out, put her fingertip on a tear in the corner of my eye, and then brought it close to her face.

"The shepherd in the storm," she said. "That's who you got it from."

She looked at me with adoration, seeing some strength in me that I wanted to live up to, and climbed into my lap. We made love. It went on and on, maybe for thirty or forty minutes. Maybe an hour. Slowly subsuming each other.

The following afternoon, I finished the drawing—the vulnerable eyes contradicted by her flipping me off—and it was the most compelling work I'd ever done.

Before the paint was dry I took a photograph of it with Anaïs's phone. I still hadn't gotten a new card. I sent the photo to Janet, with a message explaining who it was.

eighteen

I contemplated a second drawing, inspired by images of Anaïs floating down the river. While I let the idea marinate, Anaïs doodled away on her iPad, mapping out her school project. It was a small structure, "a love nest," she called it, which would theoretically stand in the middle of the river. Her class wouldn't meet until the end of the fall term when they'd each make their presentation. Every year, her professor chose three students as candidates to be considered for a summer internship at one of the biggest firms in Paris. "It's something I want," she said firmly.

Soon she had worked through the basic mechanics, pages upon pages of formulas, scratched out on graph paper and sometimes on her iPad. I enjoyed watching her lose herself in that abstract realm, so far out of my reach.

The next morning, I started on the second drawing. Rendering her in water was difficult and I pushed her hard. In the drawing, her black pubic hair was again prominent, a kind of symbol of her vitality and femininity and her kinship to the forest, with her body bleeding into the water. Something about the way she clutched her hand over her eyes, though, the elbow bent toward the sky, fending something off, was what made the picture resonate. I realized that in the past, before she was in my life, I would have minimized the hand over the face, the taut, bent elbow, perhaps even dismissed it altogether.

I brought her into the room and showed her the new piece. She studied the portrait for no more than ten seconds and said, "It's time to show Bernard."

"You think it's good enough?"

She nodded emphatically.

"I owe it to you, Anaïs. Everything you've helped me see."

She took my hand. "I love this about you," she said with a slight smirk. "Not *too* greedy."

But, still, I was greedy. Greedy for her affection and validation, and concurrently for anything she could give me to make my work ascend; and this was how she was telling me that it was okay.

nineteen

Standing with her back to us, Anaïs turned around, the corners of the drawing hanging from her fingers. With the ceiling shades open, ambient sunlight wafted down through glass panels, canted toward the north, Bernard had explained, so that it only caught indirect light, which now illuminated the portrait I'd made of her floating down the river. The viewing room, a sort of atrium, used to be part of the living room. Bernard had built a rock-and-mortar wall, opened and lofted the ceiling, and painted everything but the sandstone floor white, turning the back third of the space into a gallery. It was embarrassing to see my work next to a Bartoli, Dequene, and Genis—the Small Masters.

Bernard pressed his calloused fingers over his eyelids, pulling at them, before blinking and approaching the portrait. The Doberman was at his side and hadn't paid any attention to me when I'd arrived with Anaïs, licking her and squealing for her affection.

Now Bernard edged up within millimeters of the drawing. He turned his head so that his ear was parallel with his shoulder, following the line where her body met and sometimes melted into the water. He took three deliberate steps backward and studied the portrait from there.

"Who represents you?" he said, taking another step back, squinting at the drawing as if uncertain.

"No one at the moment," I said.

He looked back at me in surprise.

I shook my head. He returned to the portrait and his shoulders slumped.

Here comes the bad news, I braced.

"Wine or tea?" he said, moving toward the kitchen, the Doberman trailing him.

Anaïs and I followed him under an archway, crossing into a fully loaded commercial kitchen. Large stoves and ovens and heavy-duty cupboards with dozens of pots and pans ranging every size. As if to mock all the pyrotechnics, he flipped on a small electric kettle for the tea.

"I'm going to open a bottle of wine," he said, moving toward the back of the kitchen. He stopped in front of a cast-iron gate and the Doberman circled around him while he rummaged a key from his pocket. He unlocked the gate, vanishing down a stairwell that I assumed led to the cellar, but the Doberman didn't follow; instead he sat on his haunches in the middle of the doorway, blocking entrance.

"He's more serious about his wine than his paintings," I said to Anaïs.

"It's a statement."

She pulled a tea bag from a drawer, a mug from a hook, poured in the hot water, and steeped the bag in it.

"He was a very good painter like you," she said, "but never recognized."

I groaned with empathy.

"Yes, it drove him mad. Now he has tremors so he can't really paint, which I believe is a kind of relief for him."

"What are tremors?"

"In the hands. They shake if he tries to hold something steady."

"I didn't notice."

The iron gate clanged and Bernard appeared, held up a bottle. "Let's celebrate your fine work."

After he poured two glasses, during which I took notice of his trembling fingers, Anaïs lifted her tea mug and we all clinked.

"Unfortunately," he said, "I only sell old stuff; otherwise I would makes some calls about your work. They won't listen to me if it isn't from the dead."

"I'm just grateful that you like it."

"This is a good attitude." He took a long swill. "It's quite risky for an American to draw like Schiele, no?"

I nodded. "Been called lewd, sexist, even misogynistic."

"Ces connards," he called out like a bear roused from his cave. "But if I sign it Hockney or Saville then they would swoon with accolades."

"Of course," I said, wanting to wrap an arm around his shoulder.

"Yes, the artist must be good," he told me. "But at the top, who gets in and who's left out, well, that's up to the devil." Bernard brushed away the grey hair above his forehead. "See the horn growing?" he said, laughing. "It's from doing business with him for too many years."

"At least you're doing business," I said.

He lifted his wine glass. "I'll drink to that . . ." He took a healthy sip. "You've been at this for how long?" he asked.

"Since I was a kid, really . . ."

"Who got you into it?"

"My grandparents. They took me to an Andrew Wyeth retrospective when I was eight or nine, probably because I was always doodling, and my parents wouldn't really notice or appreciate something like that. So I blame my grandparents for leading me down this road." I smiled to belie any lack of gratitude.

"Wyeth was severely out of fashion back then," Bernard said. "I remember the critics lambasting him for doing those paintings of some woman in secret . . ."

"The Helga paintings," I chimed in. "He met her when she was the nurse for a dying friend who lived on a farm close by."

"I recall that even Wyeth's wife didn't know about their secret sessions that lasted twenty years . . ."

"Twenty years?" Anaïs exclaimed.

"Unbelievable . . ." I said, "His wife, who ran the business end of things, seemed remarkably understanding though. She said that his work with Helga was 'the well' to which he repeatedly went for the visual and emotional power he needed for his other, public work. Wyeth never let anyone watch him paint. *I don't want to be conscious of myself,* he said in some interview."

"Did you try to imitate Wyeth after you saw the show?" Bernard asked rhetorically, one artist to another.

I flashed him a knowing look. "Then I moved on to the usual suspects. The only one that threw everyone off was my Schiele phase. Still, it got me into CalArts."

Bernard rested his big bear paw on the top of my head, his fingertips flinching before he lifted it off. "Our paths are not so different. But," he raised his pointer finger, "you're young and you've struck on some very good fortune." He steered his eyes across his nose over to Anaïs.

She made a face, playing what I guessed was the French gangster, leaning back with her elbows on the countertop, mugging it up, more anachronistic and therefore farcical than it needed to be, a facet of French humor that I never fully connected with. It was nevertheless endearing and I laughed.

"What are you working on now?" Bernard said.

"Well, my gut tells me there's another level or two to what I'm doing. What that means I'm not sure. I'm searching. But I feel that it's just around the bend, you know."

"This is exactly what I felt when I was in the cellar getting the wine, thinking about the portrait. There's something waiting to happen. One more step and voilà."

A quick gaze like a parent to his prodigal son and then he poured the last of the wine. Anaïs snuggled closer, the two of them sandwiching me, the man of the moment, and we talked about the history of Grez-sur-Loing where many of the well-known Impressionists had come to paint. It led to stories of his brother and him hunting in the surrounding forest and fishing the once-trout-filled river.

"It's a little paradise," I said.

"Yes, that's why I've never left."

twenty

The next day, boosted by Bernard's vote of confidence, I worked hard, making dozens of sketches, harboring the secret hope that he might eventually show my work to some of his clients.

Anaïs posed for me, relaxed and easy in her body language; even her skin appeared smoother, expressions more supplicant. We held hands at every opportunity, moving from the willow tree to the stables, from the stables to one of the big windows in the house, and then curled up together for a nap in a hammock slung between two trees at the river's edge.

Clouds moved in and the evening descended with drops of rain, a hint of fall. We ambled hand in hand across the lower lawns and up the back stairs entering through the back patio. In the kitchen, Anaïs closed the window against "the fucking grey," but I loved the change. "It was fresh," I argued. Just like the change in me, now that I was beginning to believe in myself again.

She didn't eat anything at dinner and I asked her what was wrong. She rested her eyes on me, as if that was enough of an answer.

"Tell me," I said.

"When it's grey like this, and I have something to lose, it makes me crazy."

"What do you have to lose?"

Ever so faintly I discerned a sour taste in her mouth as she stared at me with an implied superiority that I didn't like. I sighed, letting her know that there was an easier, more direct way to get to the bottom of whatever was wrong. But that wasn't how she worked.

She stood, her face pulled into a grimace, and marched up the stairs.

Am I supposed to go after her, or does she want to be alone? I wasn't sure. Even if I chased her down, what would I say when I got there? Her sudden mood swing, followed by her abrupt departure, was an unsustainable way to communicate, much less resolve our differences, and I didn't want to yield to it.

Taking my time, I hand-washed the pots and pans, the dishes and utensils, and I towel-dried them and put them away. Rain beat on the stone windowsill and I saw the dark outline of the willow tree swinging in the wind. I'd light a candle for her and we'd talk and then make love sheltered from the storm.

The third-floor-hallway lightbulb was out. I fumbled between the walls until I found the bathroom and switched on that light. A white rectangle fell into the hallway and I made my way toward the dark room on the end. Easing onto the bed, I felt her body, curled into a ball. Folding around her, I whispered in her ear. "Talk to me. I want to know what's bothering you."

She didn't respond. I didn't let go. After a while, her skin turned cold and her body had become no less rigid. I faulted myself for not leaving her alone, for pestering her. I stepped out of the room and into the hall, looking for another bed.

A hard object struck the back of my head. An acute throbbing in my skull. I turned, glimpsing the cell phone Anaïs had hurled at me on the floor.

"Where is this violence you promised?" she yelled, standing naked in the hallway. "I thought you would kill for me."

"You want violence?" I said, dizzy, feeling the tight knot swelling on my head.

She spun away as I charged. Grabbing her by the armpit and hair,

I lifted her off her feet and dropped her down on the wooden floor. The thud, meat and bone against the wood, startled me for a moment. I'd never grabbed a woman, much less thrown her to the ground.

"You only want me for your work," she snarled.

"That's not true," I said, my head aching, her snarl sending a disorienting signal.

"Why did you leave me?" She thrust her chin at me.

"I thought you wanted to be alone."

"No . . ." You idiot.

Her body was limp, sprawled across the floor, with one knee jammed against the stone wall, eyes wide and alive. She wanted to be taken. No matter what, she seemed to implore, no matter my mood or mixed signals, you need to cut through all the noise and ground me.

That easy smile, rare for her to give, washed over her face.

"Show me that you want me," she taunted.

I lowered on top of her and went as deep as I could. She glared at me, vexed, insulted.

"Make me yours, Nathan."

I thrust harder, kissed her ravenously.

"No," she said. "Prends-moi le cul . . ." Her Gallic timbre gave it an eloquent ring, but the translation left no doubt about where she wished to be claimed.

twenty-one

Afterward, we lay in silence and I craved a hint of gravity, any sort of boundary, something to define us, this new territory.

"It's because of spending time in Brittany with my father's mother," she offered. "It was always grey and he would leave after a few days. Maman refused to come because Grand-Mère was a real bitch to her. I would be stuck there, alone in her dreary house, with that ugly sky, for weeks." Her hand tightened into a fist. "That's why I hate the grey."

Piecing together her train of thought, I asked, "It reminds you of being abandoned?"

"Worse. I can remember what it was like to be unloved."

Grey skies and old houses brought back the dark feelings for her. Like those times when I was hit with a wave of sadness just from watching an older man walk across the street or sitting at a bench—Grandfather—but it didn't make me erupt like it did her.

Rolling onto my side, I faced her. "Why not just tell me this before it gets out of control between us?"

"Maybe I need you to see it, to go through it with me a little bit."

I recognized how a violent argument with your lover ending in sex could bring you closer together, but here there was something else at work. I felt myself crossing a threshold, where my intimacy with how abandonment must feel for her—the disorientation and loneliness—allowed me to converge with her experience of it. She'd had the courage to take me there, and now I had an empirical understanding of an important part of her. From the outside, we must look crazy, I pondered, but from the inside it felt authentic and vital.

She rested her palm on my forehead.

"Thank you for giving me both," she said. "I know it must be difficult to possess me and to let me be. It's a rare gift you seem to have."

Then she wound herself around me.

twenty-two

I lost track of the time. We made love seemingly all night and all day. Had only a few days or more than a week gone by? Somewhere in between, I guessed. We made love in the kitchen, on the wooden deck, the lawn, in the river, the horse stables, and we were both raw, but unable to stop, unable to resist each other.

I attempted to work again, culling through the recent sketches in pursuit of stripping down the barrier between the artist and the model, two lovers melding, scraping bones. Unable to grasp it, I revisited the overhead sketches of her on the deck, eyes tracking me, a sweep of caramel and cinnamon and the two islands of black hair. But none of the forms revealed anything original or undiscovered, and I knew something was lost. My faith was kept alive by the sprawl of her attention and uncharted terrain, and the new world I found in its wake—the antithesis of rejection, of failure. No doubt a good drawing would soon materialize.

Nothing came, and by the end of the week, I was beginning to worry, preoccupied by the fact that Janet hadn't responded to the photos I'd sent of the two portraits. I tried to keep the anxiety to myself and drank an entire bottle of wine with dinner. Then Anaïs presented a chocolate mousse for dessert.

"What's the occasion?"

"It's our last night alone. Maman and Papa arrive tomorrow."

I forced a smile. She slid the dessert under my nose.

"Are you upset?" she said.

"I just wish we had a little more time to ourselves."

"That's why I need you to be strong," she said, and clutched my wrist. "Like the shepherd in the storm, okay?"

I didn't understand what that had to do with her parents' arrival, but I nodded.

twenty-three

After I finished the chocolate mousse, we drank another bottle on the back patio. Loosened up, I let out my frustration about not being able to come up with a new portrait and about not hearing back from Janet.

"Maybe you need to diversify," Anaïs said. "So all your eggs aren't in one basket."

Diversify? As in start finding a new career? I gave her a harsh look.

She was undeterred. "I've always wanted to have my own business, something that I could control. And now you have inspired an idea. Bernard is going to help me create a business selling high-quality reproductions of famous paintings." She reached across and filled my glass. "There's huge demand for this from major hotel chains, luxury cruise liners, interior-design firms, even the royal family buys this stuff. And I plan to open a shop in Paris."

I leaned back and turned away, staring at the tinsels of light on the river. It didn't even give her pause.

"Would you be interested? You're so gifted you could paint them in your sleep."

Was this something she'd had in mind from the day we met in Paris? Was this the long con, the reason for our affair in the first place? My jaw clenched because, either way, it was proof that she didn't really believe in my own work.

"It wouldn't be in lieu of your work," she said, reading my

mind. "Just a way to make some money so we can live how we want to live. Free. And it would take your mind off the portraits so ideas can flow again."

"I thought you wanted to be an engineer."

"I do. Having my own business will allow me to choose which firm I want to work for when I graduate, and I won't be beholden to some asshole."

Her resourcefulness, drumming up a practical solution to the potential roadblocks ahead, put my petty brooding into perspective. I'd been wallowing in frustration without any alternatives, without looking at it from different angles, and I kept coming up against the same unsatisfying results. Maybe I really did inspire her, this business venture—she certainly inspired me. Isn't that what truly mattered?

"Okay," I said, "Let me think about it."

She kissed me and then handed me her cell phone.

"Look . . ."

On the screen was an email from Janet.

Hi Nathan. The portraits look wonderful. You've found something that is yours, that has real emotional pull, and Gary—her famous sculptor boyfriend—says you're onto something big. Keep up the good work and have fun with your gorgeous friend. I can't wait to see where this leads.

Xo Janet

A gasp leapt out and I checked the date of the email. It was from three days ago. Now my eyes shifted to Anaïs. Without the slightest wrinkle of apprehension, she said, "I was worried that once you had what you wanted, you might leave."

Before I could respond, a horn beeped outside.

"That's Bernard . . ." Anaïs said, taking my hand and pulling me off the cushion. "My parents must be here . . ." She guided me inside, past the hearth, through the dining area, and into the kitchen. As I trailed her down the uneven stairs, I grabbed the railing, off-balance from too much wine and the rush of anger about her obvious manipulation to get me to make reproductions for her. But it was an inappropriate time to get into an argument and then she was pulling me outside.

Bernard was standing with his cigar while who I assumed was her mother and father lifted their bags from the Citroën's trunk.

"I honked to warn you, in case," Bernard said, lifting his bushy eyebrows and laughing.

Anaïs kissed him on the cheeks and I nodded, still irked, and he tipped his head at me as Anaïs towed me to her parents.

The father wore a navy blazer over a white collared shirt and Italian leather shoes, and I immediately regretted not wearing a nicer shirt. He was conspicuously dressed like Henri and had nearly the same length hair, similarly parted on one side. It was much darker and he wasn't as lean as Henri, more barrel-chested like Bernard, but their likeness suggested something crudely oedipal at work.

The mother was fair-haired with pale blue eyes and stood an inch or two taller than Anaïs, with perfect posture and feet splayed like a dancer. She must have been at least forty but she looked younger and was in good shape.

"You're a day early, no?" Anaïs said to her mother as she kissed her on both cheeks.

"Must we change our reservations, madame?" was the mother's response.

With a dismissive head toss, Anaïs turned, kissed her father on both cheeks, and introduced me. Jean Luc cocked an eyebrow at me before smiling warmly and shaking my hand. His fingers were thick, his palm meaty.

"And Maman," Anaïs said, gesturing to her mother.

She remained fixed on her mother, who craned her neck toward me and waited for me to kiss both cheeks. Touching my unshaven face to one cheek, I made the kissing sound and moved past her mouth, the same as her daughter's, to the other cheek.

"I have a name too," the mother said, and Anaïs sighed. "It's Sophie."

"Enchanté, Sophie."

"You were doing housework?" she asked, scowling at my shabby T-shirt.

"No," I said, demurely.

"Ah," Sophie intoned—the same way Anaïs often did. "We should be thankful that you wore a shirt at all."

Bernard and Jean Luc laughed, a bit nervously.

Anaïs interjected. "He was cooking over the hot stove."

"He can't stand up for himself?" Sophie quipped.

The two women seemed to square off, eyes measuring each other's expressions—Anaïs unexpectedly flustered, Sophie overtly insouciant—as if they were getting ready to duel it out.

"Let's go inside," Jean Luc said, marching the bags toward the entrance.

Anaïs turned away first, a kind of concession, and followed her father, and I quickly fell in behind her.

"So you found an American boy that can cook," Sophie called from behind us. "Bravo. It's some kind of rare species, no?"

Everyone laughed and I was laughing too, but I wondered about their banter, its echo of hostility—difficult to sustain without someone finally reaching a breaking point.

twenty-four

I offered to whip up some more spaghetti Bolognese, as there was plenty of food left. Sophie said no but Jean Luc overruled her. Anaïs helped them carry their bags upstairs and Bernard stayed with me in the kitchen, where I got to work.

"She likes to take the piss out of you at first," Bernard said, "but then she's off your back. A little test."

"Lots of tests," I said.

"Oui, you have to stand up to her but without being rude."

"I suppose it's a good way to get a read on someone."

"Efficient," he said, taking a long draw on his cigar.

He watched me stir the roasted tomatoes and garlic into the meat.

"Has Anaïs mentioned her business idea?" he said.

"Yes," I said testily.

"You're offended?"

"Seems like you two kind of buttered me up, you know, so I'd go along with it."

"Ah, you don't think I really respect your work, is that it?"

"How can I really know now?"

He took another long drag on his cigar. Looking at me or through me, hard to tell. Then he watched the smoke as it trailed out his mouth and spun upward.

"Often the difference between a successful artist and another talented but lesser-known one is how they handle the doubters," he said while watching the smoke dissipate. "What I or anyone else thinks really doesn't matter. You either make art or you don't. That's all there is. That's all you ever really know for sure."

Although it felt like another manipulation, it also rang true.

"If I were to do it, I wouldn't be giving up my own work. We'd have to be clear about that."

"Of course," he said. "I'll get some more wine."

Stepping toward the landing, he stopped. "Hey, I meant to ask you the last time I saw you, what were you doing spying on me from the river? Why didn't you come say hello?"

That was a few weeks ago. The man with the binoculars had vanished into the forest so he would've only seen me. Should I deny it?

"I didn't have anything on and you were with someone. I think it was a woman," I lied. "Hard to tell from way out in the river."

"Ah, I thought you were some kind of voyeur." He guffawed and lumbered down the stairs.

Anaïs returned to the kitchen with her father. She handed me one of my nicer shirts. I put it on while her father inspected the sauce, sniffing it up, and glanced into the boiling pot of pasta. Anaïs set three places at the massive table, using the fine silver and china for the first time. Five minutes later we were all sitting at one end of the table, while Bernard, Jean Luc, and Sophie ate Bolognese and we shared the wine.

The men complimented the food and Sophie raised her glass, first at Anaïs and then at me.

"Merci," she said.

"De rien," I said.

Jean Luc and Bernard immediately plunged into a heated conversation, which I gathered was about French politics, names and concepts that were impossible for me to follow. Sophie waved her hand in their direction and addressed me.

"Anaïs says you are a painter."

"Yes."

"And she is your model?"

Although I was still irked about her manipulation, it didn't change what she'd given me, and what Janet had reacted to so positively.

"More than that," I said. "She's changed everything for me."

"Everything? Are you in love?"

Anaïs jumped in. "Maman, don't try to scare him."

Sophie slid her eyes over to me, demanding a final verdict.

We'd never used the word *love* before. We had spent only a few weeks together, and yet the intensity Anaïs generated in me, the way it fixed my mind on her and fomented such raw emotions and, in turn, fueled my work, was more than just attraction—it ran deeper, and I was just beginning to discover how deep.

"We're definitely falling," I said more adamantly than I may have felt in that moment because intuitively I knew not to let her mother sense any waffling.

Anaïs's eyebrows flitted upward and her mouth curved. She got out of the chair and sat in my lap, clamping her arm around my neck as if to claim me.

"When do we get to see these portraits?" Sophie asked.

I deferred to Anaïs.

"In the morning," she said, without looking at her mother, kissing my neck and giggling. "It's time for my dessert."

Sophie sighed. Out of the corner of my eye, I saw Jean Luc watching his wife and then his eyes moved to me. His face was difficult to read—either lost in thought or maybe something venal flickering behind his eyes—before he glanced once more at Sophie and then resumed his conversation with Bernard.

"Bonne nuit," Anaïs called, getting out of my lap.

I stood and they all turned and looked at us.

"Don't you want the cheese?" Bernard said.

"No, merci," Anaïs said. "À demain."

"À demain," they responded.

Anaïs pulled her hair back, elbows out, gathering it into a pony-tail as she walked toward the stairs. The men were already talking again, but Sophie was watching me and for some reason I dared not meet her eye.

twenty-five

"I think I'm going to have to pass on your offer," I said as we entered the bedroom. It was a little stress test, just to see how she'd react.

"Really? Why?"

"Copying other artists' work stirs up too many bad associations for me. I'd be moving backward. Pas bon."

"Ah, oui." She kissed my cheek. "We'll have to find someone else."

She took off her clothes. I watched her, unable to detect anything unnatural or forced in her behavior, and although I'd pored over every part of her body dozens of times, as an artist and as a lover, her curves and polished skin quickly consumed me, commanding all my attention.

She glanced over, just for a half second, enough time for her to see my hunger, and all she had to do was lie back on the bed and open her legs.

Throughout our love affair, Anaïs would call out only at the moment of climax. Tonight she moaned loudly when I ate her, yelling graphically for all to hear, and that was before we made love. The last thing I remember was coiling around her and feeling her hand cup my balls—a custom she followed almost every night afterward.

The next morning, the door burst open and Sophie was standing in a leotard and Anaïs's hand was still clutching me, the room awash in sunlight. I turned away from Sophie while she admonished Anaïs, who was still attempting to open her eyes all the way. I eased onto my stomach and stayed motionless.

"Why have you invaded my room?" Sophie was yelling at Anaïs.

"Bonjour to you too," Anaïs retorted.

"The paint smell is toxic," Sophie continued. "It will take hours to air out."

Anaïs propped herself up on her elbows, stark naked in the room full of sun, and glared at her mother in the doorway. Sophie's legs were long and exceptionally taut, her stomach muscles visible through the white leotard, shoulders and arms rippled with sinew.

"You're jealous of the portraits?" Anaïs asked.

"Don't be ridiculous. Now please move his materials out of my studio. Merci."

Sophie's head then shoulders then feet pivoted 180 degrees and she moved out of the doorway and disappeared down the hall. I heard footsteps climbing the stairs to the top floor.

Anaïs turned and looked out one of the windows. "She wishes she were the muse."

"You think so?" I asked with astonishment.

"Of course. And the gouache doesn't smell compared to other paints; it's bullshit."

She was right about the gouache paints. "Well," I said, "if it would smooth things over I could do a quick—"

"Don't you dare," she seethed.

"No, no. Doesn't matter to me," I said. "Is she a dancer or something?"

"Was . . ."

Anaïs got off the bed and went out of the room without putting any clothes on. "Viens avec moi," she said from the hallway.

I put on jeans and a shirt, wavering between leaving her alone with her mother or going to watch them duke it out, with the chance I might get caught up in the mother's wrath. I took my time climbing to the fourth floor, listening for loud voices, and finally walked into the room on the end.

Anaïs was standing beside her mother in front of the two portraits that hung from the wire. Both women turned and looked at me. Anaïs was agitated, mouth tight, eyes flared open, and Sophie was calm and collected, hip cocked to one side. The moment—mother and daughter, one nude, the other thinly veiled, tussling for some kind of prominence—imprinted itself at the forefront of my mind.

"She thinks it's vulgar," Anaïs said.

I blinked, storing away the indelible image, as Anaïs approached, rolling her eyes.

"He's made you an animal," Sophie said. "Is that how you see her?"

"No more than anyone else," I said.

"It's quite crude, in my opinion, but perhaps that's à la mode."

"I'm sorry you think so," I said, wondering why Anaïs needed her mother's approval when she'd already gotten her uncle's far-more qualified one.

"At least they're not ugly like those Lucian Freuds," added Sophie.

"Let's see what Papa thinks," Anaïs said, brushing past me and out of the room.

I knew I should follow her, out of loyalty, but hesitated and glanced back at Sophie.

"Are you well-known in the states?" she asked.

I shook my head.

"Well, you're still young," she said, and walked past me, down the hall.

From the end of the hall, Anaïs called, "Wait until Papa sees them before you move them."

I waited in the room, alone with the portraits, and kept revisiting that burning image: mother and daughter, their friction like waves of heat rising off a desert floor. The idea gurgled and mutated, looking for direction. Oedipal. Primitive. Who would win out? Dominate the light? There was a natural order that Anaïs wanted to accelerate and that Sophie seemed to want to defy. Then Jean Luc appeared in a white tennis outfit. Anaïs wasn't with him. He looked refreshed, younger. His legs were thick like his torso. He walked up to the portraits and began nodding right away.

"You're a real artist," he said.

"Merci."

"I thought it was just to attract the woman."

"That's how everything begins, right?"

"Mais oui."

"Is it strange for you?" I gestured to the portraits.

"No. My mother was an artist and so is Bernard. I'm used to it. The body on full display."

He looked me up and down, clearly appraising my physique. It made me uncomfortable and I turned and unclipped the portraits.

"Sophie wants me to work in a different space," I explained, and I started out of the room.

When I passed by him, he put his hand on my upper arm. It was like bumping into a wall, stopping my forward motion.

"Anaïs is a man-killer," he said with a flash of the eyes. "You have to really"—he made a fist—"stand up to her. You understand?"

I nodded.

"Good." He patted me on the shoulder.

I nodded again and hustled the drawings out of the room and down the hall.

It may be true, but why would he say that about his own daughter?
I reflected, descending the stairs. Was he trying to scare me away or
was it friendly man-to-man advice?

I carried one last load of materials into our bedroom and Anaïs
was slipping into a black-and-white tennis skirt. I set it all down next
to the portraits in the corner.

"What did Papa think of them?"

"He was impressed."

Her cheeks went flush. "You don't mind if I play tennis with
him, do you?"

"When will you be back?"

She grinned, pleased by my longing. "In a couple hours. We'll
have lunch together. I don't get to see him very often."

I squeezed her hand. "Enjoy your time."

I walked her to the kitchen and she kissed me at the landing
before trotting down the stairs.

Peeking out the kitchen window, I watched her slide into Bernard's Citroën, her father behind the wheel. Their family dynamic
seems pretty volatile, I told myself. Best to proceed cautiously, keeping an eye out for landmines.

The car went through the open gate and climbed the small hill
before slanting with the road out of sight. Just as I was turning from
the window, a black-clad figure on a black motorcycle appeared
from a cluster of trees at the top of the hill. He was wearing a helmet
with a visor. The bike darted into the center of the road and disappeared in the direction of the Citroën.

Is he following them, or had he pulled over to fix something on
his bike, to make a call, any number of logical explanations?

Then Sophie entered the kitchen, wearing her leotard.

"Thank you for clearing out my studio," she said, filling up her
water bottle at the sink.

"Pas grave," I said, and I went for a swim.

twenty-six

My legs and arms felt lethargic when I climbed out of the river. And trying to gear up for work, I was unable to focus, exhausted, as if I'd been through an extended trek across a glacier. Had only one night and a morning with her family drained me to the point that I needed to take a nap just to get through the upcoming lunch?

Dragging my body up the stairs, I got into bed.

When Anaïs entered the room, I woke up. It was already early afternoon—I'd slept for two hours. She was rosy cheeked and shiny with perspiration. She kissed me and her mouth found my ear.

"Did she try to flirt with you?"

"No."

"Did you see her?"

"Not really. I passed her in the kitchen."

She studied me, finally nodding with satisfaction, and then stripped off her skirt, changing into linen shorts.

"Lunchtime," she said, and she walked out the door.

I lay there, unable to move for a moment.

When I got to the table, they were all seated in front of plates of turbot, a moist, flat fish that Sophie must have prepared while I'd been sleeping. I thought the men always prepared the meals? Anaïs sat on one side of Jean Luc and made no eye contact with me. Sophie, on the other side of Jean Luc, had the severe look of a ruffled aristocrat.

"Sorry to make you wait," I said.

"Don't be sorry," Sophie said. "It's already done."

I was surprised it was such a big deal to be two minutes late, but it was part of the experience, learning this new culture, and I took a seat next to Anaïs.

Sophie motioned toward the wine in the center of the table. "Would you be kind enough to pour?" she said.

"Sure." I leaned over and grabbed the bottle and filled hers first, to the brim, and then Anaïs's and then Jean Luc's—who I noticed was sitting back, watchful.

Placing the wine down, I glimpsed Sophie in my periphery. Her mouth was parted, face long, looking at me with trepidation. I glanced around to see if I had spilled or knocked something over. Anaïs was suppressing a smile.

"Did I do something wrong?"

"We must look like thirsty dogs," Sophie said. "It's obvious from the drawings that you see us as animals."

"What happened?" I asked. "I'm confused."

"If you fill the glass to the top like this," she said, lifting hers so that some wine splashed onto the tablecloth, "then it suggests that we are desperate, that we are worried there won't be more. It should be your pleasure to serve us three, four times."

I glanced at Anaïs. She tilted her head and shrugged.

I turned back to Sophie. "It's the total opposite in the states," I explained. "If you don't pour a full glass, then it seems like you're holding back. It's considered ungenerous."

"Let's eat," Jean Luc announced, and on cue the women turned their attention to the food.

Anaïs and I would normally eat fast, with our hands, but now she was cutting small pieces of fish and spearing them with her down-turned fork, then gently nibbling them off. She sat with perfect posture and dabbed the corners of her mouth with the white linen.

Jean Luc kept glancing between his wife and me, as if examining our rapport.

"It's incredible," Anaïs told her mother.

"A bit overcooked," she rebutted.

"No," Anaïs countered. "C'est parfait."

"What do you think, Nathan?" Sophie said.

All eyes were on me. It was a loaded question. I was being forced to take a side. Jean Luc's face was animated, eyes dialed with expectancy, as if this was all for his entertainment.

"It's awfully good," I said.

"C'est parfait?" Sophie insisted.

"Nothing's perfect, nor should it be," I said.

She drew her chin down in deference and lifted her glass. "Well done."

I lifted my glass, only to notice Anaïs glaring at me. I'd slipped up already—sharing even this trifle moment with Sophie—and I cringed inside anticipating the arduous balancing act that lay ahead.

"So who won the tennis match?" I asked Anaïs without skipping a beat.

"Papa of course." She rested her hand on his shoulder. "He was the star of the Sorbonne. I have no chance."

"No, no," he said. "Anaïs is very fast, with a deadly serve. It's always a challenge. Do you play?" he asked me.

"No. Love to watch though."

"It's too civilized for you, perhaps?" he said. "I mean with the lines and the fence around you. It's not vast like the Alps."

"Never thought of it like that, but you're probably onto something."

"Sophie's the same way." He glanced at her. "That's why she dances and is bored by tennis."

"Where did you two meet?" I asked.

"I saw her dancing in *The Sun Princess* at Ballet de l'Opéra de Paris," he said.

I turned to Sophie. "You were a professional ballerina?"

She combed back her blonde hair and nodded.

"She *is* a ballerina." Jean Luc shot her a debonair look. "Magnifique."

Anaïs rolled her eyes, chewed on the side of her tongue, and stared across the room, tuning them out.

"Maybe, at some point, she'll give us a little performance," he continued.

"Only for you, chéri."

"Do you still dance for the ballet?" I asked.

"No, no. I stopped many years ago. I do some consulting for them and a summer training, but nothing more."

"But you must tell him why you stopped," Anaïs cut in.

"Well, I became pregnant."

"Nineteen years ago."

"Anaïs feels guilty," Sophie said. "But she really shouldn't."

"It's still difficult for her to give up the light," Anaïs sniped.

"It seems that you're threatened because I've kept myself up, and men still look at me."

"He's not looking at you," Anaïs said, gesturing at me.

"I'm not talking about him."

"You mean Henri?"

"No. I mean men in general."

"Well, Henri followed you around like a dog and you loved it."

Sophie glanced at Jean Luc, a certain tautness in her cheeks that I wished I could've recorded—raw disdain or perhaps regret, I wasn't sure. But Jean Luc would not meet her eye. She took in air through her nose, her mouth pressed closed, and her eyes flinched with near hatred, and then it all evaporated and she turned back to Anaïs.

"We were guests in his home. Should I have ignored him?"

"You were eating it up."

"I did nothing. Besides, if you want the man not to be like a dog, then you should become a lesbian. That's my advice."

"You went out on the boat with him, Maman. You were gone for an hour. He was completely spaced out when you got back. Lost somewhere."

Jean Luc slammed his fist down on the table. Everyone snapped to attention. "Arrêt!" he barked. "We are here to relax. I've been working nonstop for six months. I need some peace. Tu comprends?"

"Oui, Papa."

"Oui, chéri."

His command, swiftly taking control of the situation, recalled the scene in the hallway when Anaïs demanded that I ground her, claim her, and I suddenly inferred how any man she was with would be inherently tied up in her oedipal drama.

But you're older and wiser than Henri, I argued. And it's just part of the package she comes in. Besides, Anaïs and I are both artists at heart, a much better fit.

twenty-seven

After lunch, Anaïs and I took a long walk through the forest. She knew where the woods opened up and led me through its shaded corridors and exposed meadows. We held hands. No words exchanged. Some of the leaves were half yellow now, mingling with a few rusty ones, and the sun was already lower in the sky, casting shadows on the grass cushioning our feet, the shrubbery scraping our shins.

She ran her fingers through my hair, gathering it up. "I love walking with you like this," she said. "You don't put any weight on things. Your lightness is good for me."

My face scrunched up.

"What?" she asked.

"Well, I can always feel your weight."

"Well then . . ." She swung around behind me and jumped on my back. "If I'm going to be the burden anyway, I might as well get something out of it."

She made me carry her all the way to the river. We plunked in the tall grass and I was surprised she didn't want to make love—a simple "not now."

Closing my eyes, that burning image of Anaïs and her mother in the upstairs room resurfaced. Still amorphous, all friction and light, two bodies at war, and I would need to see them together again in order to discover what it meant.

Good luck orchestrating that, I thought, and a quake of frustration went through me, as if I were already lamenting the loss of something important.

"Tell me about your sister," Anaïs said, breaking the silence.

My relationship with Alice was still a sore spot and I'd mentioned her only in passing. My body retreated deeper into the grass. My hesitation drew Anaïs out of her sunken patch and she propped on an elbow, watching me.

"Alice and I look a lot alike," I began. "But that's pretty much where the similarities end. She went to Stanford. Has a law degree. Works in D.C. for the State Department, doing who knows what. She sort of sided with my father when I decided not to pursue a career in law. I left the University of Washington, moved to Venice Beach, and started at CalArts. It wasn't an explicit falling-out. Just a slow fade. She's married now and has a young baby so she's busy."

"Do you really see your relationship with Alice like a fact sheet?" Anaïs asked with exasperation.

"What do you want to know?"

"How did you become so close? Not all siblings are."

I glanced at Anaïs, wondering how she knew that Alice and I were once very close. The shape of her eyes reminded me again of the agave leaf, a fluid, enveloping line—one of the ways I would evoke her ineffable potency when I finally did another portrait.

"Alice was my first muse," I said.

A sound of excitement rose up Anaïs's throat.

"We were in high school," I continued. "Even though she was beautiful and sixteen, she was still a bit of a tomboy and hung out with my group of friends. I'd been drawing for years, copying other artists' styles, and at some point I started doing these rough portraits of her at the fort we hung out at. It was my first truly original work. All my buddies, who only seemed interested in sports and video games, were suddenly into the portraits, and Alice was very encouraging, so it was an exciting breakthrough for me.

"Anyway, I entered the portraits in an art contest and I won. But some art critic for the local paper wrote that he was *disturbed by the prurient gaze between the artist and model, brother and sister.* It started some nasty rumors about her, about us. Kids would stare at her in school and make comments.

"My mother and father never said a word until one day my father decided that Alice wasn't allowed to hang out with me anymore, giving no explanation other than *She needs to make her own friends.* Alice suffered a lot that year. Got totally ostracized. And I was no comfort because I was the cause of it all. She sort of went into a shell and didn't seem to come out until college.

"Our relationship got a little better at that point. I'd visit her, she'd visit me, but there was always this undercurrent of animosity she had for my art. She never wanted to see it and would sort of minimize my pursuit of it. Then when I bailed out of university it all came to a head."

Feeling a warm pressure at the backs of my eyes, I stopped talking. I could feel Anaïs studying me and then she rested down beside me, shoulder to shoulder.

"So," Anaïs said, "it is to Alice that you want to prove yourself."

"Yes, you're right," I said, staring into the overhead limbs. "I wished Grandfather was still alive during that time, someone to talk to. I even tried to conjure up that soothing feeling of being out to sea with him by going fishing. But it turns out it wasn't the sea that did it, it was him."

A few tears rolled down my cheeks. Anaïs turned her head. I let her watch me, allowing her to see the unfiltered emotions that I'd never shared with anyone but her and Grandfather, and perhaps, for a short time, with Alice. The side of her face was cradled by the grass, and her skin radiated the soft golden light falling down through the limbs, no judgment in her face, her father's *man-killer* unrecognizable. She rested her palm on my chest, her fingers faintly kneading.

"You've seen all my ugliness," she said, motioning toward the château. "It's okay to show some of yours."

twenty-eight

Dinner was pleasant, without drama. I wondered if each of them had gotten the hostility out of their system. After a lively backgammon round robin, won by Jean Luc, we went to our rooms.

Anaïs and I were very slow and deliberate, all the hunger contained, seeping out our skin, mouths, fingers. We never separated, unwilling to peel apart, and I fell asleep inside her.

In the morning, I watched her, black hair curling like flames across her face, lips peeled outward in soft sonorous exhales. I wondered how she ever got into engineering, so meticulous and inanimate, compared to her impassioned personality. Later, when she awoke, it was as though she'd heard my thoughts, and she brought me outside to show me something.

The driveway split where the horse stables ended. One arm of the driveway curved to the front of the château, right up to the big entrance door, and the other arm went around the back of the house, turning into a dirt track. Anaïs led me around the back and onto the track, stopping beside two circular woodpiles that looked like giant beehives.

"It's called a Holz Hausen," she told me. "It's a special way to stack wood. I'd read about it in one of Papa's magazines when I was twelve and it piqued my curiosity."

She pointed to the older, less-stable circle of wood, held up with crooked limbs leaning against its sides.

"That was my first attempt. But the instructions were in German and I didn't catch some of the technical terms. See how, as the sides get higher, the wood begins to tilt a little more outward?"

"Especially near the top," I said.

"Yes, well, they should tilt slightly inward; that way if pieces fall they fall into the open center. This one"—she pointed at her first, rickety attempt—"would collapse right onto the road without the wood posts holding it up."

She moved to the newer, sturdier-looking Holz Hausen and patted it as if it were a prized stallion.

"This was my second attempt and the one we still use. See how I put in some small perpendicular pieces of wood every meter or so, so that the pile tilts inward?"

I nodded.

She walked around to the backside of the older pile—her first attempt—and I followed her. There was an opening where some wood had collapsed, and she stepped over the pieces and into the hollow center of the pile.

"I would come here when I was upset. It was my secret hideaway where nobody ever thought to look."

Her face turned into that twelve-year-old girl—rounder, plumper, eyes full of wonderment—and she sat down in the center. Tilting her head back, she looked up at the sky. "It still kind of works," she said in a woebegone voice I'd never heard her use.

twenty-nine

Finishing their croissants and coffee, Anaïs went upstairs to put on her tennis clothes, and Sophie went to her room, I assumed, to put on her leotard for her workout. Jean Luc watched his wife climb the steps, studying her as he sipped his coffee.

"I'd like you to do a portrait of her," he said.

He must be joking.

But he raised his eyebrows, expecting an answer. Was this a test of my devotion to Anaïs?

"Well," I said. "Anaïs wouldn't like that."

He folded his lips, dipped his head to one side, eyes searching the kitchen.

"You do it on the side," he said. "I'll pay you well."

How well? I was almost out of money and running thin on materials.

"I'm not sure that's such a good idea."

His eyes narrowed and he glared at me, the intruder who'd settled in his house.

"So you refuse?"

Eyebrows forked down, he dared me to disobey him, and I felt the immense power he held over me. It was his house, his food, his daughter; everything I'd come to rely on for my art was under his control.

"It's such a complicated situation . . ." I said, getting up and moving to the sink for a glass of water.

"Pas grave," he belittled, like a man that expected to get what he wanted, and I turned to tell him that I needed to think it over.

Footsteps startled me. Anaïs was trotting down the stairs, racket in hand. She kissed me, told me she already missed me, and then as they started down the entrance stairs, Jean Luc peeked back and gave me a thumbs-up.

thirty

I heard the gate bang shut and stood in the center of the kitchen. What exactly was behind the threat of his forked-eyebrow glare? I'll poison your relationship with Anaïs. Interfere with the work. Kick you out of the house.

What the hell was he planning on doing with a portrait of his wife? He couldn't let Anaïs see it; she'd know it was mine.

Picturing Anaïs discovering the portrait, stabbing it with a chair leg or a knife, gave way to that image of mother and daughter in the upstairs room. This time, they turned and looked at me, jockeying for attention, willing to go to any lengths to outshine the other, and the shapes presented themselves more lucidly—a visceral, perhaps decisive painting that had been looming at my fingertips, but always out of reach.

This could be a blessing in disguise. How else would I ever get an opportunity to work with Sophie and explore the validity of that image? I stepped toward the first flight, then stopped. You're letting yourself get lured into a highly volatile situation, I warned. You need to pause and think this endeavor through.

But a soft thud followed by a pitter-patter trickled down from somewhere above, and I felt a spike of adrenaline as more lines appeared in my head.

Go swimming, I told myself, while climbing to the second floor. Go swimming, I repeated, as I climbed to the third and fourth.

I peered down the hallway at the room on the end, and a foot rose to the center of the doorway, covered in a ballet slipper. Seconds later, I was knocking on the wooden doorframe.

"Oui?" I heard Sophie's voice.

"It's Nathan."

"Entrez."

I stepped inside. She was on the floor, stretched over one leg, holding the toes. She looked at me, waiting for me to declare why I was there.

"Your husband mentioned doing your portrait."

"Ah," she sighed. "Yes."

I waited. She seemed to be thinking it over. "Well," she said, "let's get it over with."

"I'll get my stuff."

When I returned, Sophie was looking out one of the windows, watching something outside. She turned, waiting for instructions.

"Would you mind just dancing or whatever you normally do?" I said.

She shaped herself into what she told me was the classic first position: heels together, legs straight, back perfectly erect, arms hanging, slightly bowed, and hands facing each other with tensed fingers in front of her thighs.

I took down the lines. Asked her to turn so that the light fell on her a different way. I did some shading and thought about Anaïs. Not particularly intrigued by Sophie, I asked her to try another position.

By the third position, I worried that she was all style and form. Detecting none of Anaïs's undercurrents or contradictions, she seemed too polished. Probably good enough for Jean Luc's portrait, though. Just knock it out and collect your money.

"What's wrong?" I heard Sophie's voice.

I looked up. "Nothing," I said, feigning nonchalance.

I went through the motions of drawing her, while the tedium and disappointment of witnessing a promising idea as it crumbled, literally in my hands, grated on me, and soon I was counting out the days, the weeks now, that I'd gone without discovering anything good.

"Shall we take a break?" I said, expecting that a swim or a bite of food would rejuvenate me and help me finish off Jean Luc's assignment.

In one fluid motion Sophie stepped out of her pose and walked across the room and out the door. I glanced at the sketches, hoping I'd find something previously unseen, but they remained flat. Just pretty pictures.

When I returned from my swim, she was in the kitchen making lunch, sipping a glass of white wine. I offered to help with the lunch but she shook her head.

"I'm curious," I said, "did you really stop dancing because you got pregnant?"

"Oui. I'd spent my life going after this goal of prima ballerina, and then in five minutes, as long as it took to do the take-home test, I gave it all up."

I noticed Sophie's hand around the wine glass, the tendons along the top like piano strings lifting the skin, thickening to cables along the forearm—slightly grotesque juxtaposed to the small classic features of her face.

"Please don't move," I told her.

Next to the telephone there was a cup full of pencils and some scratch paper and I used them to get it down. The sketch was a first crack, a blip of hope that she might reveal something deeper.

"When do you think we'll get another chance to work?" I asked when I was done.

"Oh, you'll see. She'll be off with Jean Luc every day now. When she gets to have him she uses up every second," she said. "By the way, I stored your work in a trunk upstairs under blankets."

I nodded. "Thank you for sitting for me."

With a tart smile she said, "Not for you. For Jean Luc."

thirty-one

A gain, I had to rest before facing the lunch.

When Anaïs came into the room to change, she immediately asked if Maman had tried to flirt with me.

Looking into her eyes, my neck muscles tightened and my jaw strained to open, releasing a choppy laugh.

"I heard her cooking down there, that's all."

"I'm surprised," she said, as if dumbfounded that her sense of the situation could be so off.

It made my lie seem bigger and now I felt even crappier.

"I miss working with you," I said with affection. "You're my lucky charm."

"Not lately . . ."

"That's not your fault."

She'd taken off her tennis clothes and was stepping into her shorts. "Do you have something you need to say?"

My hands were clammy all of a sudden. Had Sophie made some sort of suggestive remark to her?

"No," I glanced around with incomprehension. "Why?"

"You seem . . . different . . . preoccupied . . ."

I shrugged. "I'm in a funk. That's all."

The lunch was dominated by a discussion of the new bakery in the village and whether or not the croissants were as good as the old bakery's. The instant I caught sight of Sophie, prickles of discomfort went up my chest and I stopped looking in her direction. Then I noticed Jean Luc scrutinizing me and worried that Anaïs would pick up on the underlying vibrations and become suspicious. Although the session with Sophie was a dud, it was already nagging at me, and I took a long pull of wine to calm my nerves.

Anaïs pushed back her chair and the screech startled me. She got up and went to get the cheese from the fridge. With her back turned, Jean Luc glanced at me, perking his eyebrows, and then at Sophie. Well? he seemed to ask.

I remained stone-faced and waited for Sophie to respond. She nodded and one of his cheeks dimpled with satisfaction. What the hell was going on? It still didn't make sense.

After lunch, I couldn't wait to go outside and be alone with Anaïs, away from her parents, as if drawing her would help cleanse me of my deception and the dreamlike strangeness of whatever it was that I'd allowed myself to get mixed up in. Drawing her lounging on the deck, I kept dropping my pencil and screwing up her contours. Back and forth, I debated whether I was betraying her trust or simply doing what Jean Luc was forcing me to do. My pangs of conscience wouldn't shut up and I cut the session short.

"I've got too many ideas racing through my head right now," I told her. "I should probably just spend a few days figuring it out."

"So I *have* lost my charm," she said as I gathered the materials.

"No, no. It's going to be over in a few days."

"What's going to be over?" she asked with suspicion.

"My block."

That night, for the first time since we'd consummated our relationship, we failed to make love.

thirty-two

When she left in the morning with her father, I decided that I'd do only one more session with Sophie, finish up quickly, and hand over the portrait to Jean Luc by the following day. If he didn't like it, he wouldn't have to pay me—better than living in duplicity. I didn't have the nerve for it, or so I thought.

When I entered the studio Sophie was warming up, wearing a black leotard and pale rose tights. Without a word to each other, I set up and started taking down her lines. She moved in a mesmerizing flow and I captured her in pieces, working fast, and after about twenty minutes, I had enough to make a portrait for Jean Luc.

"Are you getting what you need?" I heard her ask.

I looked up. Her head was dipped toward me, a mien of genuine interest.

"He'll like them," I said.

Her mouth puckered, eyebrows flinching, as if mildly offended.

"I'll have something by tomorrow," I added, gathering up my materials and moving them closer to the back window where the light was better now. I'd pick out a couple suitable sketches and get right to work on the portrait. As I set my stuff down, a noise, fabric ruffling and snapping, got my attention. I turned around.

She was peeling off her leotard and tights. Her skin was almost ivory and it caught the light well, standing out against the backdrop of stones. She set her feet wider than her shoulders, squatting until her thighs were parallel with the floor. She bent forward, letting her arms hang down from her shoulders, propped on fingertips. She lifted her heels so that she was balanced on the points of her ballet shoes. She looked like a spider, elegant but deadly.

Each ligament and strand of her sinew flexed and strained, stripping her of those refined social pretenses that seem to stifle the flesh, her predatory nature unchained. I was drawing furiously, breaking pencils, flipping pages, and everything else in the world had melted away. I was alone with the peculiar white spider.

At some point I'd stopped working and was just watching her. Propped on four legs, she embodied her animus, some kind of shamanistic transformation. Where did this come from?

Face puffy and red with gathering blood, breathing out of her flared nostrils, her hamstrings and buttocks began trembling.

"Have you got it?" she grunted.

"Yes."

Slowly she lowered her heels to the floor and sat down, torso dripping with sweat. Her ribs expanded and contracted while she caught her breath. Pulling out her hair-tie, she shook free her braid and I wanted to run my fingers through the wet strands, taste her warm ivory skin—No, it was just the thrill of the moment, the image, don't confuse the two.

The room was quiet but for her breathing and she seemed to be waiting for me, sitting there, having just revealed some deep-seated, primitive identity, as if she'd turned herself inside out.

"That was amazing," I said, still feeling turned on. "Thank you."

"It's for Jean Luc, remember . . ." She rocked to her feet. "If you want me to hide the drawings, please put them with my things."

Leaving her leotard on the floor, she rolled her neck, crossed the room, and strode out the door. I was already filling out and piecing together the sketches in my head, wanting to somehow evoke her feral power through the pores of her skin, and her damp leotard drew me across the room.

Lifting it off the floor, I brought its crotch to my nose and inhaled. Inebriated by her scent, a flood of images—hunched on four legs, ivory skin encasing threads of muscle, the pale blue eyes, a miasma of shapes and colors—triggered an unsettling bloodthirsty vision of she and I eating each other like cannibals, until I heard the wooden gate scrape open.

thirty-three

Anaïs arrived with her father and a young woman, her friend Valerie. Valerie looked younger than Anaïs but was in fact a year older. She was shy, the shrinking violet to Anaïs's blooming sunflower. She had short blonde hair, a small button nose, and round, naive eyes. Since I didn't need her for a few days, Anaïs explained, and was preoccupied with coming up with a new idea, she'd invited Valerie to keep her company.

Uncle Bernard also joined us for lunch, fresh sardines in lettuce cups and a risotto that I made. The risotto wasn't as al dente as I'd hoped but no one complained.

It was another unseasonably warm day. Bernard opened the windows and laughed ironically when he told me it had snowed a meter in Chamonix, where he had a chalet.

"It's the first early winter we've had in the Alps in a decade," he cheered.

Hiding behind the notion that visions of powder snow were lulling me away, I let myself dip in and out of the drawing I was conjuring of Sophie—a spiderlike figure, the elegant predator, and then a horrible thought intruded.

Jean Luc had, effectively, commissioned me to make the portrait. And if it turned out to be as good as anticipated, I would never be able to hand it over. Never.

"Where are you?" Anaïs said.

"Thinking of all that beautiful snow."

"Ah, you had that look like you'd found a juicy idea."

"I wish . . ."

After lunch, the girls hung around the house, making it precarious for me to look over the spider sketches, and I took a walk in the forest. The sky was a pastel blue, streaked with a few inert clouds, and a breeze rustled the treetops. Sophie might be my Helga, I reflected, marveling how Wyeth's secret muse had not only produced great portraits but also informed so many of his other paintings. Working in secret with Sophie was like living in a world where boundaries had no eyes, making it easier to trespass thresholds. The thrill of exploring the darker edges of myself through Sophie, something I would've never even considered indulging before I'd arrived at the château, had me in its grip and was all I wanted to do.

But how would I deal with Jean Luc? He'd expect his merchandise.

Then I wandered into a meadow and the answer came to me. Make a second portrait from the ballet poses—I could do it in a day or two—and then when Anaïs leaves with her father in the mornings you can work on the spider idea.

thirty-four

Breakfast. Anaïs told her father she wouldn't be joining him for tennis. I thought I'd lost another day to work on my secret drawing, but after our morning swim, the girls went to the village to pick up sausages for lunch.

Sophie was gone too, perhaps with Jean Luc, and I trotted into our bedroom to grab my materials and take them upstairs where the secret work was hidden. Anaïs had left her phone on our bed and I decided to write Janet, let her know I was closing in on another piece. Opening the email icon, I saw a new message from her, dated yesterday. From the first line it was good news.

She had a show starting the last week of November, about three weeks from now, running through December, and wanted to include me with the other two artists—*well-known and hot at the moment*—but I needed a third piece, *something that takes the Anaïs portraits to the extreme*, and I'd have to ship them to L.A., which would take a week.

"Hell yes!" I raised my arms and jumped around the room.

Then I deflated: That means I have only a little over two weeks to find and execute a drawing. And it sounds like she wants it to fit with the other two portraits of Anaïs, meaning the spider mother won't work.

I read the rest of Janet's email. There was a gallery in Paris that she would arrange to professionally crate the drawings. *Don't roll them up because it'll take a week to ship.* Unfortunately I'd have to pay for it because the show was already way over budget. It could cost as much as a thousand euros.

> *No problem,* I wrote back, so there'd be no doubt that I had something for her. *I'm working on a piece that fits right in with what you want. Thank you for considering me. Please send the Paris gallery info.*
> *Best,*
> *Nathan*

I dropped the phone on the bed, gathered all the Anaïs studies from the pile in the corner, and rushed upstairs. Unearthing the drawing pad hidden under blankets in an old trunk, I tore out and spread the Sophie sketches across her studio. Then I shuffled through the Anaïs studies, looking for ones that might fit with the spider. I stalked around the studio, arranging and rearranging mother and daughter beside each other, hunting for a powerful coupling. In my mind there existed a sort of magnetic confrontation, what I'd seen broiling between them on more than one occasion, *something that takes the Anaïs portraits to the extreme,* but right now it wasn't there on the paper. You have to be patient, I told myself, and also be willing to accept that your vision for a double portrait might be a pipe dream.

"Les saucisses girls sont de retour à la maison," Anaïs's playful voice echoed up the stairway, and I shut all the drawings away in the trunk.

thirty-five

Finally Jean Luc stood, ending the lunch, and I gestured for Anaïs to follow me. Out of everyone else's earshot, I told her the news.

"And I've got a great idea for your next portrait, which I need to get started on right away."

"Super . . ." she pronounced it *sue-pear*, seemingly delighted that I needed her again.

While she explained to Valerie that we were going to work alone for a few hours, I retrieved my materials and then met her on the back patio. Taking her downriver, we crossed the partially sub-merged beaver dam to the far side. Searching out the tallest grass, I found a patch directly across from the château. The tips were turning a mustard color and a few oak and beech leaves were shedding in the wind. Her hair was pulled off her face, leaving it nicely exposed, and I asked her to lie on her back.

"Now turn and look at me."

The grass bent around her body, outlining her form in bladed spheres, and I imagined the spider mother at Anaïs's feet, then on each side of her, but without Sophie there, the correct orientation proved elusive.

"I might need someone to be a sort of prop," I suggested while I worked, easing toward breaching the unmentionable.

"Valerie will do it."

"I need someone taller. Hey, what about your mother?"

Her arm fell across her breasts and she snorted, shaking her head. "You can't wait to get her naked, can you?"

"No. I'm searching for something intense, like Janet asked for."

"So I'm not enough?"

She got to her feet. Reached for her shirt.

"You're more than enough, Anaïs . . ."

I grabbed her arm. She slapped me across the face. It stung but I didn't let go.

"Wake up, Nathan," she seethed. "You think you can just ask her to sit for you and that's it?" Her mouth quivered ever so faintly. "No. With her, everything is complicated, treacherous. I'm telling you right now she will destroy everything."

Her eyes were bursting with a confluence of rage and grave warning, smoldering. Please don't do this to me, Nathan. Please.

Her reaction seemed out of proportion to anything I could imagine her mother really doing, but it didn't matter because Anaïs was convinced.

"Okay," I said. "I get it . . ."

She ripped her arm out of my grip and cast her eyes to the ground.

"I'm sorry," I said. "Valerie will be fine."

thirty-six

Anaïs worked on her school project for the rest of the afternoon and evening, and I borrowed Bernard's Citroën for a run to the art-supply store in Fontainebleau. After I paid, down to my last hundred euros, I wondered if I had enough time now to spend a day churning out a portrait for Jean Luc in order to put some money back in my pocket.

After dinner, Anaïs and Valerie put on a French movie, a comedy, and the humor was lost in translation. In the middle of the night, I woke up on the couch and when I went to our room, Valerie was in the bed, so I slept in my old room.

Bright and early, I woke up eager to work on the third piece. At breakfast, Anaïs announced that she and Valerie were going to take on Sophie and Jean Luc in doubles tennis. I gave her a look of consternation.

"Don't worry," she quipped, rubbing her palms together, "it will be a short match."

That got the banter going between them and I knew I would just have to wait until after lunch.

I tried to work on the portrait for Jean Luc, pretty ballet poses, but was too distracted by the feeling that time was running out on me; and because he knew about art, I couldn't do something half-assed. One drawing after another, I shredded them, until my pencil became a nub.

Near the end of lunch, I had to contain myself from moving around in my chair while waiting for Jean Luc to finally go take his nap. When he stood up, I immediately corralled Anaïs and Valerie across the river. It was just after two o'clock and already cooling and every minute spent trying to get the girls to explore various positions felt like years vanishing.

"Would you stand just to the side of Anaïs's head?" I told Valerie, motioning with my hand.

Anaïs was lying in the grass, and Valerie put one foot beside Anaïs's head.

"Can you sort of squat like this, like a spider?" I told Valerie, showing her by example.

She did her best to assume the spider, but she wasn't supple enough, diminishing its power. Unprompted, Anaïs rolled onto her side and rested her cheek on top of Valerie's foot, as if it were a pillow, wrapping her arms around Valerie's ankle. Her knees tucked in, sort of spooning an imaginary partner, all the more pitiful for the solitary foot under her cheek.

"Stay there," I told her.

I went after her lines from multiple perspectives. Sweat was dripping down my temple, tickling my ear, and I wasn't sure how much time had passed when I noticed Anaïs looking up at me, grinning.

"It's beautiful to see you find it," she said.

"It's beautiful to see you smile." I kneeled beside her. "You just gave me the magic lines . . ."

I kissed her and it felt like eons since we'd last touched. She pulled me down on top of her and we rolled around, until Valerie cleared her throat.

thirty-seven

The girls and I stayed up late that evening, sharing a few extra bottles of wine. Privately I was celebrating my discovery and couldn't get it out of my head. Of course I'd have to see the Anaïs-Valerie studies alongside the Sophie sketches, but I believed I'd grasped that dynamic confrontation first glimpsed in the upstairs room.

Around midnight, I plugged my phone into the stereo, playing Led Zeppelin's *Physical Graffiti* album. The women were skeptical when I started dancing and they both laughed at me. But I pulled Anaïs off the couch and moved her hips until she gradually succumbed. Valerie joined in. The wine had relaxed her and she lifted her arms in the air and rolled her hips. We all whirled and gyrated around each other. The women paired off and I sat back and watched. It was erotic fun, but after a few minutes I was thinking about Anaïs and the double portrait again, and Valerie was in my way, blocking my line of sight. It was a preview of how her continued presence would hold up the work, not advance it. I had what I needed and working with another figure was no longer useful. How many days would she stay? How many days would be lost? I barely had two weeks.

The blinders came down. A Machiavellian calm washed over me. I saw where I needed to go and Valerie was in my way. I rose from the velvet chair and cut between the two girls. Facing Valerie, I moved in closer, furtively glancing to see if Anaïs's eyes would congeal with spite. I rolled my shoulders and slinked within inches of Valerie, and she made the fatal error of running her finger across my mouth. Anaïs's eyes twisted up and one hand knotted into a fist—her boiling point. On cue, I yawned and said good night.

thirty-eight

Anaïs woke me up just before noon to let me know she was driving Valerie to the train. The smile I shot her, cool and precise, gave her pause, and I said, "I like having you all to myself."

"Ah, you must be feeling really confident about the new portrait."

"I am . . ."

I took her face in my hands and kissed her hungrily.

"Ooh la la," she sang out. "He's turning into a monster. But I like it . . ." And she sauntered out the door.

Per my routine, I jumped in the river and swam vigorously upstream. At the bridge, I rolled onto my back. The sky was blue, the air relatively warm, and I drifted, buoyed by the weather's good omen. Until I heard the whir of a motorcycle.

I swung my feet down and looked up at the bridge. The railing eclipsed most of the bike, but it looked like the black-clad driver I'd seen come out of the cluster of trees a few days ago. As he crossed to the middle of the bridge, the bike veered closer to the railing, and I saw someone sitting behind him, her long, raven-black hair falling from her helmet down a yellow dress. The engine wound up and the bike shot away.

Was that Anaïs?

Ridiculous. She's dropping Valerie at the train.

I'm not even sure it was the same guy.

Then something moved in the trees along the riverbank. I thought of that bird watcher with the pale face. Was he spying on me? His shadow darted past tree trunks, tagging limbs, and then he popped out.

It was a large deer, antlered. Black eyes blinking down at me. He turned and pranced back into the forest.

Afloat in the river, hemmed in by the woods, I was a sitting duck, exposed. As the current swept me around the sharp bend, the château came into view, its long rectangular windows like hollow eye sockets, watching, its myriad rooms suddenly feeling like a maze with no exit.

Relax. It's all in your head. Just stay focused on your work. You're almost there.

thirty-nine

When I reached the levee, Sophie was lying on the deck, sunbathing. I got to my feet and stepped around her in my wet boxers. She smiled at me, reached up, and opened her hand. Impulsively, I took it. Her hand tightened around mine and she rubbed her thumb over my knuckles.

"Great hands . . ." she said seductively, and I gave her an ambivalent smile. "You're freezing. Come lay in the sun with me . . ."

Glancing back at the wooden gate, checking the road rising behind it, I eased down onto my stomach. The warm planks burned against my chilled skin, and I rested my cheek flat on my arm.

"We can hear you two at night." She was on her side, facing me. "Did you know that?"

"I wondered . . ."

Her eyes pulsed. "I like to imagine it's me."

I felt blood rush into my cock. Thankfully I was on my stomach.

She reached out and combed the wet hair off my forehead to the nape of my neck, gathering it up and squeezing it. Water dripped between my shoulder blades.

"Stand up," she said.

"I'm still getting warm."

"Please. I won't ask anything more."

Her blunt, sultry gaze got the better of me, reaching down to the core of the animal, and I sat up on my knees. I felt myself straining against the wet boxers. With her eyes grazing along my shape, her free hand clasped her ear, pulled and massaged the lobe. Then she glanced upward. I followed her eyes to one of the second-story windows. It reflected a blue piece of sky and a silver-rimmed cloud.

"I have to prepare the lunch," she said, and she stood up.

She collected her sarong from the railing of the footbridge, wrapped it around her waist, crossed the drive, and walked through the door.

What was she after? Was it part of her competition with her daughter? I glanced up at the second-story window again. What does she have against me? Well, you're not French and you're not rich, with an unstable future. A mother's worst nightmare. Maybe that's it. No matter, her little dalliance might have led to something more, become the final straw, destroying my relationship with Anaïs and therefore any chance of finishing the third piece for the show.

When I entered the kitchen, it was empty. No food out. Nothing in the oven. She's probably getting dressed before she starts the lunch. On my way up the stairs to the third floor, I mulled over how perilous my relationship with her was becoming, and I flashed on the second-story window—the reflection of sky, cloud, and was that a tree limb? Too high for a tree limb—and that stopped me in my tracks. It was her bedroom window. Someone had been standing inside, watching us.

Tiptoeing to the second-story landing, I heard hushed voices echoing in the hallway. I crept toward the sound. The voices were seeping through the middle door. I stopped outside and put my ear to the wood.

"You want him, don't you?" Jean Luc said with lurid anticipation.

"Oui."

"How would he fuck you?"

"From behind."

An instant later, I heard Sophie sigh. "There we are, chéri. Like a young bull."

A mattress spring squeaked and the bed frame thumped against the wall.

forty

I t was some kind of arrangement; it had to be. The threat of other men, perhaps younger men, had become a kind of aphrodisiac for him, I surmised, and maybe for her as well. They'd been married twenty years and I wondered how long it took them to get to this point. The various perversions to excite them, to allow them to stay together.

Lying on the bed that I shared with Anaïs, I thought over the riddle. She didn't seem aware of her parents' erotic game, at least not the details, but its mere existence would be felt and probably contributed to her conflicted feelings about her mother.

Abruptly, my love affair with Anaïs turned unfamiliar, as if I were just meeting her now. No longer sure of what we had, I questioned how real or imagined our relationship had been all along. How much she truly believed in my work, if she had simply planned to use me for her reproduction business with her uncle, all of it, and it brought back those eyes in the forest, the bird watcher and his binoculars, the voyeur in the bedroom window, being swept along in the river's current, susceptible, trapped in a maze. Although she feared her mother's seductive prowess, she'd invited me to the château. Why? Was it part of some larger scheme? Or was it only about showing off the portraits in order to remind her mother of everything she'd given up? And did Sophie really need the attention from younger men? Or was the game only for Jean Luc's benefit?

It was like a gale-force wind whipping the world into a frenzy in my head, a blizzard of questions. Despite the chaos, one thing stood out, clear as a bell: I was a pawn in the service of the Blanchon family.

But if I walked away, I'd be sacrificing the double portrait and all that it promised. I'm the only one that loses in that scenario. They go traipsing on and I have to start over, hoping not to fade into obscurity. No. I couldn't bear that.

Much like losing myself in a drawing, the intricacies of the Blanchon puzzle consumed me, and instead of taking a step back, I wanted to know more, see more of *the ape beneath the clothing*. The deeper I comprehended them, the stronger the double portrait would turn out. It was all fuel for the fire. A fire I would need to complete my work.

forty-one

When Anaïs returned, I was in bed under the covers, sapped of energy. No longer propped up with curiosity, I'd given in to some sort of flu.

"Are you feeling sick?" she asked, and I realized that Anaïs was wearing a white blouse and linen shorts, not a yellow dress like the girl on the motorcycle.

"I feel like I'm coming down with something."

"Oh, baby. Let me make you some tea."

"Wait . . ."

I patted the bed. She sat beside me and I watched her, trying to read her face for signs of deception.

"What is it?" she asked.

"Why did you invite me out here?"

"Because you were cute and your work showed promise."

"And I could do some reproductions for you?"

"It crossed my mind, but anyway you rebuffed me. Honestly I was more interested in having a little fling and forgetting about Henri."

"And your mother? Didn't you realize, on some level, that my portraits of you would stir things up between you two?"

"I can't spend my life worrying about her reactions."

"It seems like you were trying to provoke her."

Her eyes shifted, pondering. "I suppose I was. Your age is halfway between Maman and me. I guess I wanted to see if I could keep your attention, your devotion." She smiled down at me.

"Is that what all of this is about for you?"

"No. But now you make me see that it was a part of it."

There was no hesitation or halting manner to her answers, nothing defensive in her tone, which made it difficult to discern if she was shading the truth. A lot to digest. I closed my eyes, weary in mind and body, forming my next question carefully.

"Once you've proved that you're more desirable than your mother, what happens to me?"

She rested her head on my chest. "We've gone way past just sort of using each other. Way past that . . ." she said.

I wanted to believe her. There were so many reasons to. A feeling of tenderness overcame me, declaring itself in opposition to the cold, manipulative Anaïs I was suspicious of. She was ambitious and independent, and I'd always admired her for it, found it refreshing, so penalizing her for that now would be hypocritical. Maybe she does have an agenda, but so do I.

I brushed a few strands of black hair over her ear. Ran my palm along her back. I couldn't imagine not being with her. The only certain deception between us was my drawing her mother in secret, and now the double portrait I was attempting to craft under its cover, a second secret. How do you reconcile that? I asked myself. You have no right to question her motives.

She lifted her head off my chest. My face softened and I smiled weakly.

"I'm going to rinse off before we work, okay?" she said.

"Of course . . ."

She walked into the bathroom. When she closed the shower curtain, vanishing, I wondered how we'd maintain our romantic relationship and continue to work together without Sophie and Jean

Luc's dramatics interfering. A strange buzz in my head, as if being part of her parents' machinations, holding their secret, was a competing radio frequency crowding into the music I was trying to lose myself in.

"You have to tell me why you're so distraught," her voice jarred me.

I'd been embroiled in my thoughts for who knows how long and now she was standing over me, drying herself.

Tell her everything. That's the only way to go. It will set you both free.

I opened my mouth and heard a voice—*Don't mention the erotic game. Too explosive. Could scuttle getting the double portrait. Your big chance.*

"I'm worried I won't be able to pull off the third portrait and I'll miss the show," I said, omitting what had precipitated this. "And that my failure will fuck up our relationship."

She wrapped her hair in the towel like a Sikh and studied me as though from a distance.

"I have to be honest, Nathan," she said. "If you become too weak, I'll get restless and try to test you. I told you in the beginning that I needed you to be the steadfast one in the storm."

It threw me, this glimpse of the *man-killer*, and a twinge went down my arms. I nodded.

"I'm going to rest for a little while," I said.

She forced a smile, turned, and put on her clothes.

forty-two

I awoke before dinner and wandered into the kitchen. Anaïs was cooking with Jean Luc and she hardly acknowledged me.

"Maman is sick too," she said. "She won't be joining us for dinner."

"Maybe something's going around," I said without thinking.

Jean Luc and Anaïs both looked at me. Feigning ignorance, I touched the glands at my throat. "Does she have a sore throat?"

"No. Body aches."

"That's different," I said. "What's for dinner?"

"Chicken with a salad."

"Can I do anything?"

"No, no. You better just rest," Jean Luc said with an edge.

I sat down on the chair by the table with the phone. Anaïs didn't look at me, giving her father all the attention, discussing tomorrow's plans, which I was clearly not a part of. It was dark outside the kitchen window and cool drafts wafted across the room. Why did she show him so much devotion? Was it compensation for his habitual absences, a way to pretend she didn't really resent him?

Jean Luc rubbed spices over the chicken—the first time I'd seem him take part in the preparation of a meal—and I wondered if he knew I was privy to his secrets. He was certainly privy to at least one of mine, and when push came to shove, if Anaïs found out, I would be the one who got discarded.

It was strange to watch them together—cooking, talking, laughing—when I was so cognizant of his most intimate needs, the path they'd sent us all down. But, of course, I'd readily taken the bait, so I, too, was culpable. At that precise moment, he glanced at me, a silky, self-satisfied wrinkle on his lips, as if to declare, I'm the head cock. Then he broke into laughter at something Anaïs said and turned away.

I took a pencil from the mug, slid a sheet of scratch paper closer, and began drawing them. I sketched heavy leg irons around their ankles, draping the chain across the floor to the bottom foreground of the paper, where the artist's foot was then shackled too.

She stayed up late with her father and when she finally got into our bed, she lay down at the far edge.

I reached over and ran my palm over her ass. Kissed her nape. No reaction.

"What's wrong?"

"You fall apart so easily," she said with quiet scorn. "I mean, you were so high about the new portrait and then I come home and suddenly you've become sick with worry over it, and full of all this paranoia about me, us. It shuts me down."

If you only knew what was going on behind your back, I retaliated. The shit I have to navigate. But considering my involvement, I knew I didn't deserve any compassion. I rolled over.

"I'm sure I'll be fine in the morning," I said coolly.

Anaïs left with Jean Luc earlier than usual, not even a kiss good-bye. I heard the car on the clay as I walked into the kitchen. Out the window, I watched Anaïs open and then close the gate. The thinning willow tree swung in the wind. I was losing her. A hole was opening in my center. Another demonstration of how Anaïs and my work had melded into one—she could drive me to ruin the same way failing to produce the great double portrait for the show would. I slammed my hand on the chopping board.

forty-three

S ophie was sweeping the floor, prepping the room for her workout. "So how does it work?" I said.

She looked at me blankly. "You flirt with Anaïs's boyfriends and that excites him?"

Sophie showed no emotion, leaned the broom in the corner, and started to warm up. "It doesn't have to be a boyfriend of Anaïs."

"Okay," I scoffed. "Did the game start with his demand that I do your portrait?"

"Yes."

"But then he needed more?"

"Yes."

"Why do you go along with it?"

"For love," she said.

"Give me a break."

"No?" she stopped moving and put her hands on her hips, addressing me. "He wants to feel like a man and I want to feel like a woman. The alternative is he has mistresses and I take lovers or just turn into an old maid. But that's not for us. Sex is a kind of glue that has kept us connected through all our years."

"Wouldn't Viagra be easier?" I said.

Sophie stretched her arms to the ceiling.

"It's not the same," she said. "Taking a pill compared to being driven by jealousy and possessiveness." She looked me squarely in the eye. "They are completely different experiences for both of us. The pill we leave as a last resort."

"But Anaïs can feel that something is going on behind her back. It drives her crazy."

"How do I tell her something like this? Nothing would be gained. Even though she acts so sophisticated and bold, don't forget, she is only nineteen."

She had a point. The game in itself was their own private matter, and disclosing it was unlikely to bring Anaïs and Sophie closer or help smooth the seas, and would probably make things worse.

"If she learns of this," Sophie said, her eyes a sheen of blue ice, "I'll never pose for you again, you realize, and besides, Jean Luc will kick you out."

"I'm not going to say anything," I shot back. "But I don't want to be a part of it anymore."

Lifting her eyebrows and pursing her lips, she gave me a challenging stare. "Bon."

"You're screwing her up."

"Wouldn't it be worse if her mother and father had lovers or got divorced?" she retorted.

"I don't know."

Sophie went to the window and looked out. She appeared to be wishing I'd go away.

"Okay, can we get to work?"

"But I thought you didn't want to be a part of it anymore."

"I have a show coming up and I need a third piece."

She rolled her eyes, turning her head, a show of ambivalence.

"Can't we just work together without it being for Jean Luc?" I argued.

That got her attention. She lifted her chin. "Mais oui . . ."

forty-four

I led Sophie to the tall grass, carrying the studies of Anaïs and Valerie with me. I would've preferred to conceal them from her, but time was of the essence and I needed to use them to position the spider around her prey.

What struck hardest was having Sophie hanging over Anaïs with her four spider legs, while I envisioned Anaïs resting on her side, head at the pointed base of one of the spider legs, cradling it.

I worked from higher and higher points of view until I found the right angle, depicting the sinewy insect ready to smother her daughter.

"You're putting both of us in it now, huh?" Sophie said, glancing at the Anaïs studies.

I hesitated. Accessing my raw, unfiltered impulses and letting them live in the drawings was much easier when neither woman knew what the image was going to be in the end. It was like having sex in private as opposed to a public place where you could be seen and therefore come under scrutiny, losing your freedom to be true to nature.

"Can we not talk about it?" I said, drawing her mouth.

"Superstitious?" she laughed.

I nodded and turned to the Anaïs studies, her mouth like her mother's, and began to sketch her in, cradling the spider's pointed foot—a substitute for the affection she really wanted. When I got her outline in place, I saw how important her particular expression would be. The final battle between the real and the ideal would take place over the play of emotions in Anaïs's face.

"You've got your hands full now," Sophie said, "juggling all your secrets."

That killed it and I told her we were finished for the day. She left right away and I was relieved that she didn't try to scrutinize what I was working on; her reaction might make me self-conscious and protective, even for her sake.

forty-five

S towing the drawings in the trunk on the fourth floor, I heard Anaïs and Jean Luc return from tennis. Anaïs remained aloof for the entire lunch, and after the meal she stole away to the porch, napping on the cushions across from her father.

How could I blame her? I'd become perpetually distracted, ducking and weaving to keep my work hidden, all my attention directed toward the third piece for the show; and it was compounded by the fact that she was the only one in the château left to guess at some deception she could feel going on behind her back.

When Anaïs woke up from her nap, I asked her to sit for me.

"At this point, it's become obvious that you just want me for your work," she said. "That's all you talk about. That's all you worry about."

"Yes and no," I told her, taking her hands in mine. "Making pictures of you and having a relationship with you is really one thing. I need your passion, your ideas, your unique perspective. There is no one like you. No one."

"How long can that last?"

"Is that what you want, Anaïs? You want us to last?"

She gave me a feisty look. Studying me.

"Then we need to make paintings together," I said.

Her eyes closed for a moment, a rebuke; then she got up and walked down the steps toward the riverbank. But I'd glimpsed a curl at the corner of her mouth, a blush in her cheek, as though she'd been reassured that I still had it in me, a whiff of the shepherd she so wanted me to be.

She was less guarded yet still somber throughout the entire session in the tall grass, which was perfect for the play of emotions in her face. I couldn't bring the Sophie drawings, but they were fresh in my head, and by late afternoon I'd finally nailed down Anaïs's far-off gaze.

I stepped back to view the drawing. Her eyes teemed with a longing to be nurtured while a repellent flicker hinted at some underlying aggression; complex, deeply conflicted, and accessible all at once. The next step would be to draw her in over the sketch-lines at the feet of the spider, hidden now in the trunk, and marry the two figures. I was only days away from executing the double portrait.

"It's good, Anaïs," I told her, and I kneeled down. "Thank you for sticking it out with me."

I opened my arms, wanting to kiss and hug her, wrap her up with my love and appreciation for all she'd given me, all she'd sacrificed. But she rolled out of reach, got up, and walked back to the château.

forty-six

Dinner. Rain tapped the windows. Air musky. Sophie was describing a cheese monger at the open market, the way he spoke like a gangster from Marseille, and Jean Luc teased her for doing such an accurate impersonation. Apparently, when Sophie's father was a young man, he'd dabbled at being a gangster in Marseille. This revelation seemed to lift Anaïs's spirits and she perked up, asking questions about her grand-père. Perhaps hearing stories of her mother's childhood adventures touched a nostalgic nerve in Anaïs, and after dinner, without any warning, she asked me to walk with her in the rain.

We bundled up and strolled arm in arm along the riverbank. We went under the bridge and stopped at the edge of Bernard's sprawling lawn. She held my face in her hands and the warm glint returned to her eyes.

"I'm falling for you," she said. "And it freaks me out. Makes me crazy . . ."

"It's okay. I'm falling too."

"Then why don't you say it?"

"Because you're convinced I just want you for the portraits. Which is true but also the same thing as falling for you. I know that sounds . . ."

With both hands she cupped the back of my head and kissed me.

"Je t'aime," she whispered.

"Je t'aime," I said, and I wrapped her in my arms.

Just like that, by some invisible force, we were back on track. She took my hand and guided me onto Bernard's lawn. We passed the Rodin, misted with rain, and then the Claudel, and I thought we were going to consummate our affirmation by making love at their feet.

But she told me we had to wait and pulled me toward the château. The house looked asleep, only a single stain of color in one of the windows.

"Where are we going?"

"To see Bernard."

As we climbed the last pitch of grass, the door opened. Bernard raised his hand, a solemn wave, with the Doberman at his side. Anaïs picked up the pace and we walked inside, dripping water on the floor.

"I'm glad you came," Bernard said, closing the door and kissing Anaïs on both cheeks.

He flipped on a bank of lights and the living room appeared through an archway. Soft leather couches and old smoking chairs and chandeliers hanging from steel chains; a big hearth like Anaïs's with the same kind of moulding around it and silver candleholders and silver drinking cups and scattered cozy atolls of low-slung chairs in circles, some with silk pillows, all oriented toward the ten-foot-high French doors facing the lawn and river.

I glanced at Anaïs, who was admiring the room too—it was something you never overcame. Bernard lifted a bottle of port from atop an antique escritoire and poured three glasses. The gun case behind him displayed old rifles and some pistols that looked ancient.

He handed us the port and studied me for an extra beat. "I see that you don't know why you're here," he said.

I shook my head, thinking it probably had to do with Anaïs's business venture.

"Viens." He led us around to the front of a massive leather couch, and although we were wet, he motioned for us to sit, and he opened a cigar box, offering me a Cuban.

"No, merci."

"A shrewd businessman," he said. "Never celebrate too early."

"What are we celebrating?" I asked.

He lit a cigar, cheek-ballooning pulls off the end to get it going. He let the smoke trail out and pointed the ember tip toward a large marble coffee table. Resting on the white slab were four drawings made with pencil or crayon, accented with watercolor, that I instantly recognized as Egon Schieles.

"*Nude Girl with Folded Arms*," Bernard said, pointing at the one on the far left. Motioning at the labia-splayed girl in the drawing beside it, he said, "And *Observed in a Dream.*"

I was standing, stepping toward the table. My shins hit the marble. The next portrait was of a seated woman, seminude, in a green blouse and green underwear, fingers touching her chin, pale almost-yellow eyes, big almonds, staring at you and simultaneously past you—confident, witty. And beside it was *Reclining Nude, Left Leg Raised.* Her refined, classic beauty—doe-eyed with something pleading in her brow, lips pursed, the upright position of her head—in counterpoint to her raised leg, exposing her sex. The lines were true without sacrificing the idea he was after. The spare graphite against the paper enriched the emotion in a way that a thousand thick brush-strokes could never do. It was everything I aspired toward but never came close to.

"Amazing," I whispered.

Bernard's beefy fingers clamped onto my shoulder and eased me back.

"I know, mon ami," he consoled. "I know. But they're worth too much to drool on."

"I'm sorry." I stepped back and sat down. "They're just so damn good."

"But you can do this too," Bernard hailed, handing me another glass of port. "No doubt."

His bulbous nose, bear head, and watery blue eyes all seemed to smile on me with genuine compassion and affection.

"You're already doing it," Anaïs chimed in.

"Doing what?" I asked, realizing they had something specific in mind.

"Making pictures like this," Bernard said. "You're that good."

"Watch out. His head is going to really swell." Anaïs chummed it up, shooting me a coy look.

He scoffed. "But you can't deny what he's done with those portraits of you."

"So you want me to do reproductions of these?" I interrupted their ego-stroking.

"Essentially," he mumbled behind a veil of smoke.

Dropping my head back against the couch, I let out a sigh.

Anaïs put her hand on my thigh. "I know you're not comfortable doing copies, but I thought maybe for Schiele you'd reconsider."

I felt myself gravitating back toward the Schieles on the marble slab. The power of his lines seemed to reach down into my soul. Keep your eyes off those drawings. Don't lose control. Don't give anything away.

"In 1912," Bernard suddenly intoned, "Schiele went to a small town outside of Vienna called Neulengbach, where he hoped to use the peace and quiet to concentrate on his work."

Where is this going?

"Unfortunately he ended up in jail for the public display of pornographic images," Bernard continued. "He'd showed some nudes he was working on, one of which was of a local girl, to some of the townspeople and they'd reported him. After the ordeal, he cleared out his studio and went back to Vienna. However, by his own account, he made a number of erotic drawings that disappeared in the move. These four pieces here"—Bernard nodded at the marble slab—"were drawn around the same time, giving us a good idea of the sort of stuff he was doing in Neulengbach."

"So you want me to make . . ."—*reproductions* wasn't the right word and I searched for it—"drawings *like* those?" I said, pointing at the Schieles.

"Yes!" He opened his arms, gesturing toward the drawings. "You can use them as a reference, with Anaïs as your model."

"Are you offering me a show?"

His body straightened and his eyes, teared up from lack of sleep and alcohol and smoke, wouldn't meet mine. He shook his head.

"No, I'm offering you a chance to make twenty thousand euros, which will allow you to keep working on your own stuff and finally bring you the recognition you deserve," he said. "You have your big show coming up. It will be expensive to ship the three pieces, no?"

I glanced at Anaïs. She must have told him—could have even shown him the email on her phone—and now I thought about her asking me to walk with her after dinner and her sudden reconciliation, her declaration of love. Was it any less genuine now? Or just part of her puzzle?

In the moment it was impossible to delineate the various pieces, but some part of it was connected to the long con I'd suspected when she'd first brought up her business idea.

Still, I needed to make money to ship the portraits for the show, and buy a ticket to L.A., and there was no denying that having all that cash would give me the freedom to just work without the weight of survival hanging over me, a privilege I'd never indulged. I couldn't rely on Jean Luc paying me, I had nothing to give him, and his portrait proposition had turned out to be only a front for his erotic amusement.

"Why not just do reproductions, like you two originally talked about?" I suggested.

"Because we can make real money this way," he said.

I turned to Anaïs. Her hands rested on her knees. She peered up at me without cunning or ambivalence, eyes round and wide like when she'd shown me her childhood woodpile. In spite of her wiles, it was hard to pour cold water on what looked like unadulterated enthusiasm.

"What exactly are you going to do with them?" I asked Bernard.

He sat down, reclining in the plush leather. "No, no," he said. "You do the drawings. You take it or leave it. That's all."

forty-seven

Rain splattered the glass, a subtle drumroll accompaniment to our lovemaking. "Punish me," she whispered, and she opened her thighs wider, as if acknowledging her exploitation of my dreams and craving to be split in half, her penance. I obliged her; it was one of the ways we communicated.

She let out a long deep sigh and we shuddered in spasms, collapsing in a heap on the bed. A few minutes of recovery, then she rested her hand on my heart.

"I thought it would make you happy," she said. "Secure the money in time for your big show. But don't do it if it's going to cause tension between us. Okay? Love is more important."

I turned toward a breeze coming through the window. No matter the game she was playing, the manipulations, my gut told me her love was a separate entity, and therefore real—she wanted to help me find success, and help her uncle, and help herself, none of them mutually exclusive.

"He's going to sell those drawings as authentic Schieles, isn't he?" I said.

"That's his risk," she argued. "There is no law against drawing them. Only selling them."

Again, I had no other way to come up with a thousand euros, plus another four or five hundred for a cheap plane ticket, in less than two weeks, while also finishing the double portrait. The lure of no longer being at the mercy of Jean Luc and Sophie, of finally towing my own weight with Anaïs, was hard to shake, and imagining all that money in my pocket gnawed at me, sung to me, gave me a sense of floating above the fray. If I just do this one thing, which in itself is not against the law, perhaps I could be free.

forty-eight

Jean Luc had to go away on business and I wondered if that had been planned or at least encouraged by Bernard. When Anaïs and I arrived at Bernard's house, there were fresh croissants and café au lait waiting for us.

"I think you should work in the living room," he said. "Everything in there is turn-of-the-century or earlier."

"Okay," I said, understanding that every detail would be scrutinized by whoever was hired to authenticate the *newly discovered* Schieles. "But what about the paper and pencils?" I asked him.

"No problem," he said. "The previous owner of this house, a painter from the twenties, left stacks of old drawing paper, with boxes of crayons and pencils, all kinds of materials from the turn of the century, in the cellar."

Bernard got off the stool and opened the iron gate while the Doberman stood guard, and Anaïs added to the story.

"He and his mother, my grand-mère, would make their own Renoirs. When they thought they'd mastered him, they each took their favorite piece to some galleries in Paris, saying they'd discovered the paintings at an old house. Even after the gallery people had them inspected, Bernard's was accepted! Once they'd had their fun, they revealed the secret and gave the money back."

"So he's done this before," I said.

"Oui," she said sharply, irritated that I wasn't as enthralled by his hijinks as she was.

Bernard arrived with the four Schieles, passing us in the kitchen and laying them across the marble slab in the living room. I stood over the drawings, studying them, while he brought up the stacks of old paper, pencils, and watercolors for me to work with, and an easel.

"All set?" he said, and I nodded, never taking my eyes off the Schieles.

I heard him leave out the front door and when I looked up again Anaïs was taking off her clothes. She curled up in one of the smoking chairs. I gathered up the Schieles and carefully moved them to a corner couch where they could no longer intimidate me.

Making the drawings convincing will demand my total surrender, I told myself. I put a blank sheet of paper at the foot of the smoking chair and kneeled. Looking past her thighs, I studied her chin and jawline. She was looking out the French doors, presumably at the statues, lawn, river. I made some initial marks and then, as if she understood we needed some sort of catalyst, she opened her legs, grabbed my hair, and stuffed my face between her thighs.

When she was on the edge of climax, I slouched back to the floor. Stymied on the cusp, with one corner of her mouth kinked somewhere between lust and loathing, eyes wound like a bloodthirsty animal, her expression ignited me, and from there, the pencil struck the paper as if from Schiele's own hand. The lines came preordained, so electrifying that I wouldn't let Anaïs rest. By lunch, I had five drawings done and she walked out on me, heading for the river.

Bernard returned with food from the market. He saw the drawings on the floor and studied them.

"I won't sign his name," I told him.

He flung a shoulder upward. "I have someone who will do that," he said. "But I only like these two." He pointed at the more graphic drawings. "And we need three."

I glanced out the window. Anaïs was walking up the lawn, coming in from the river.

"And if I don't like the next one you have to keep trying."

"No way. I'm only doing one more. I need to get back to my own stuff, Bernard."

"I can make your sessions with Sophie quite difficult," he warned. "One word about it to Anaïs and you lose everything. Everything."

I wondered how he'd found out. Did his brother tell him, confide in him, or was it Sophie? Maybe he caught on, came by one morning when we were working, then confronted her, or told Jean Luc? In any case, now he had me by both balls. Even if I didn't care about losing Anaïs, which wasn't true, I would still need access to Sophie while I married the two figures onto what I'd come to realize needed to be a bigger surface, refining, making sure it was right, with a last chance to discover something new.

"Fine," I said, and I went to the kitchen.

forty-nine

Bernard approved the next drawing. "Almost better than Schiele himself," he said. Now I had to add the watercolor. Anaïs was angry that I didn't make love to her, *to celebrate your achievement,* but I was on a roll and there was no time or need for sex or sleeping, just for working. She left her uncle's house in the small hours.

In the morning, I showed the three finished pieces to Bernard and he grinned at me, eyebrows practically wriggling, and clapped his hands together a few times. After a quick breakfast, he brought up his largest drawing paper from the cellar, and he also offered the use of one of his easels. The easel would really help but the paper wasn't big enough for what I wanted to do with the mother-daughter portrait. Fortunately, he had to go to Paris for a lunch and offered to drop me in Fontainebleau, near the art-supply store.

He let me out on the outskirts of town and handed me a hundred-euro note, nowhere close to the twenty thousand he'd promised me, claiming that he wanted to make sure the drawings passed the test before he paid us. It wasn't part of the deal but I had no leverage.

The store was on the far side of Fontainebleau, off the beaten path of the tourist-packed streets, and I was the sole customer at the moment. I couldn't find any paper that was large enough. Utilizing the hundred euros, and the fact that the owner had seen me there before, twice with Anaïs, elevating my status above American tourist, I cajoled him into stretching a four-by-six-foot grounded linen canvas for me. It wasn't as smooth as paper but I would use its faint coarseness to suggest the women's subtle fragmentation. I had enough money left for more black and flesh-toned gouache paints, and a taxi back.

The big canvas was cumbersome. As I got closer to the center of town, where the taxis waited, it got more difficult to wield around pedestrians, so I walked on the street next to the curb.

I was approaching a wider street that was closer to the hustle-bustle when a Range Rover careened into my periphery, nearly taking me out. I turned to shoot the driver a scowl, but then I saw who was behind the wheel. It was the guy from the bridge, the birdwatcher; at least it looked like him—same straw hat and pale face.

"Get in, Nathan," he said in an American accent. "I'll give you a ride back to Grez-sur-Loing."

Something was wrong, I knew right away, and I felt the blood vacate my head, drain from my face, and fall like sand down my arms and legs, leaving my upper body hollow. All the blood seemed to lodge in my hands and feet, and they felt swollen.

"No, thanks," I said, a quavering note in my voice, as I heard the whir of a motorcycle behind me.

The black-clad figure, looking like the same one who'd darted from the cluster of trees and who'd crossed the bridge with the woman in the yellow dress, suddenly screeched to a stop a few feet away. He leaned over the handlebars of his Ducati, his ominous tinted visor seemingly urging my compliance.

"What do you want?" I said to the man in the car as I stepped onto the sidewalk, rested the canvas on the ground, and clutched it against me.

"We can't talk here," he said, taking a gold badge out of his coat pocket and flashing it at me. I could see U.S. in big letters with an eagle perched above.

"You need to get in the car and hear me out, Nathan."

Parts of me seemed to come loose. I felt drunk, his face warping like in a funhouse mirror. Then his dead, humorless eyes sobered me up. I glanced at the guy on the motorcycle. He was dismounting, and the man in the car pointed at him.

"Mr. Beck will put your things in the back," he said. "I'll drop you in the village. Just hear me out. Please."

fifty

"Hal Cumberland," he said, opening his hand for me to shake as I sat in the passenger's seat.

I nodded and shut the door. Hal pulled a U-turn and drove fast, weaving his way out of the town and onto the main road. It cut through dense woods, making it seem later in the day than it was. Mr. Beck was right on our tail. Once we were at cruising speed, Hal started talking.

"I'm sorry to accost you like that but I needed to talk to you right away."

I studied him. He looked like Colonel Sanders. He was doughy and his voice carried a midwesterner's lilt. The only threatening feature to him was the deadened eyes, milky brown and unflinching.

"About what?" I said.

"I work for the FBI. Lead man for the Art Crime unit."

It was like being in outer space, looking into a meteor shower, a thousand flaming scenarios, accusations, regrets, lies trampling through my head. I tried to use my sudden collapse into despair to demonstrate naive shock.

"So what do you want with me?"

"I was hoping you'd help me out."

"How?" I scoffed, the blood in my arms and legs quickening, rushing back.

"I'm looking for some stolen drawings. They were pilfered during an exchange between two museums in the United States about a year ago. Thought you might have seen them. By mistake, of course. You wouldn't have necessarily known they were stolen. It was only in the papers for a day."

"I think you have the wrong guy."

"Are you Nathan Woods?"

I gave him a weak nod.

"Currently residing with the Blanchon family in Grez-sur-Loing?"

"You got me," I said sarcastically.

"It seems you got yourself." He smiled.

"How's that?"

"The Blanchon brothers are of great interest to us. You're living in one brother's house, sleeping with his daughter, and maybe with his wife, so you're in a unique position to help."

I looked at him blankly. Yet the undersides of my arms and legs were pinned to the seat. I glanced out the passenger's window and flashed on that moment in Paris, walking beside Anaïs, her fingernails digging into my skin, and my intuition telling me to get away from her, that she was dangerous.

"Who made the drawings?" I said, watching the forest go by.

"Egon Schiele."

My throat closed. Luckily I was still looking out the window and I shook my head, praying he didn't notice me gasping for oxygen.

"Why won't you look at me?" he said.

I took in air and turned, exhaling discreetly.

"Why are you so nervous?"

"Cops always make me nervous," I said, telling him the truth.

He chuckled and gestured to the rear of the car, asking if the canvas was for the third piece for my show.

"Are you reading my emails?"

"Of course."

I shook my head and turned away from him.

"I really want it to work out for you, Nathan," he said.

Sure, I thought, wondering what was next, and suddenly he pulled over. It took a moment to realize that we were in Grez, on the bridge by the château. His eyes were directed over my shoulder, at the river, as if looking for a good fishing hole.

"Are you in love?" he asked.

"What does that have to do with anything?"

"Yes or no?"

I thought of her posing for me or decoding my work, holding my hand in the forest, swimming beside me in the river, the way she always made love as if it were our last night on earth, but once I came back to the present, I saw all the holes and wedges imposed by the forgery scheme and now by this.

Yet saying *no* felt wrong. I shrugged.

Only one side of Hal's mouth lifted. I detected envy or a bitter remembrance in the awkward, palsied smile.

"All I'm asking is that you call me if you see any Schieles." Hal handed me a business card. It read *Ski Tour Guiding* and had a European phone number on it. If anyone found this in my pocket it wouldn't raise any suspicions. "That's all you have to do," he said. "No one will know."

"You could be anybody," I retorted. "I mean, it's easy to buy a badge on the Internet. How do I know you're legit?"

He sucked in his breath, teeth showing. "Well, let me put it this way: if you protect them, I'm going to send you to jail, and then you'll have your proof."

"Or I could just ask the brothers if there was any reason the FBI would be asking about them." I countered.

"Ah, that would be considered aiding and abetting. I don't advise."

"You got an answer for everything, huh?"

"I've been at this a few years."

"Yeah, well . . ." I started, lost my words, and then turned and opened the door.

Light-headed, I dropped onto the bridge and went to the rear of the car and retrieved my materials. Mr. Beck was nowhere in sight. I didn't look at Hal when I passed the front of the car.

"Don't forget about me, Nathan," he called out.

I didn't take the road through the village; instead I clambered around the side of the bridge, down the embankment, and I followed the river toward the château.

When the house came into view, I started to sweat. How am I going to face them? If Hal is right then they're the kind of people who would always be on the lookout, constantly have their radar on, so to speak, and would see unease in your face, hear it in your words.

Maybe I should turn around, walk to the village, and call Hal from a pay phone. End this thing right now.

I leaned the canvas against a tree trunk. Glanced at the house then back at the canvas. Once you make the call you've shut the door. No double portrait, no show, back to square one—the best chance you've ever had, will likely ever get, down the tubes.

fifty-one

Bernard's Citroën was parked at the end of the drive. He was supposed to be in Paris. Strange. Of all the people to have to face right now, Bernard was the worst, the one most directly involved. I ducked into the horse stall farthest removed from the château, setting the canvas and paints in a dark corner next to where I'd stashed the easel Bernard had lent me. I sat on the ground for a few minutes trying to gather my wits.

It dawned on me that Hal wouldn't be asking me to snitch if he knew for sure that Bernard had the Schieles. Which means he also doesn't know if I've seen them or not. So that means I haven't been clearly implicated. Not yet. That's a huge relief. It gives me a little breathing space to map out a strategy.

What about Anaïs; how much does she know? Is she aware that the Schieles are hot? She's willing to profit off fakes; why not stolen art too?

It was as if my lungs were collapsing, to think that all her desire and affection was just an act. It was inconceivable. You'd have to be a robot. It just didn't fit. Bernard had to be manipulating and lying to her too. Please let that be the case.

Throat parched, mouth full of cotton balls, I paced the interior of the stall, hot one second and cold the next, while my mind toiled to narrow everything down and find an equilibrium. At some point, I stopped pacing, pushed open the stall gate, and walked toward the house, momentarily made sturdy by the esoteric compass of a painter who believed he was on the verge of his masterpiece.

Get the double portrait done and get out, I resolved. You didn't steal anything. You aren't selling anything. You are an innocent painter trying to make it.

fifty-two

The four of them were sitting at the dining table, plates of untouched lasagna in front of them.

"Where have you been?" Anaïs demanded. "You look disheveled."

Reflexively, I combed down my hair then stopped myself. I avoided Bernard's eye and thought it through: if I mention the canvas, she'll know what to look for later, make it harder to hide it. "Walking," I said.

"You should have told me you'd be late for lunch," she said, her preoccupation with etiquette a welcome respite.

"I lost track of time. I'm really sorry, everyone," I said. "Got a bad headache. I have to lie down. I'm sorry."

"Why should you be sorry?" Sophie asked.

"Because I held up the lunch."

"But what about us?"

I looked at her, perplexed.

"Now we can't be upset because you are. It's like guilt, which is really only a selfish way for the one feeling guilty to get off the hook."

My entire array of senses was frayed and all I could do was garner a wayward nod. It must have come off as something else, a form of awe or reverence, because Anaïs lifted up the tablecloth and sent the glasses and plates tumbling.

Jean Luc slid his chair back and Bernard twisted out of his. But Sophie remained seated, a glass of water and a brick of lasagna landing in her lap.

"Yes, Maman," Anaïs shouted, standing with the tablecloth still in her hands, "you are more sophisticated and you have more to teach him. Even your breasts are more impressive. We get it!"

Sophie flicked the debris off her lap, took a napkin and dabbed her stained crotch, and asked Jean Luc if he'd like dessert now.

"Touché," Anaïs said dryly, and she pulled the cloth all the way off, breaking whatever hadn't been broken before. She stormed across the kitchen, shedding her jeans and top as she went down the stairs and out the door.

fifty-three

My plan was to take refuge in my room, avoid Bernard and Jean Luc as much as possible, and use every spare moment to work on the double portrait and prepare my departure. Instead of going up to room, though, I changed my mind, realizing I still needed money to ship the portraits and buy myself a plane ticket.

I helped clean up the mess, hoping for a moment alone with Bernard. When Sophie and Jean Luc went up to their room, I suddenly got squeamish and had a hard time looking Bernard in the eye.

"How long till you have the money?" I asked.

"A week. Maybe two," he said. "Did you find a big-enough surface?"

I nodded and felt my hand quivering.

"Can I get an advance now?"

"What's the rush?"

"The show is in less than two weeks."

"So you have time."

"Not really. It'll take a week for the pieces to get to L.A."

"You can't wait to leave?"

"No. I'm just anxious about the show."

His jowls went slack, eyes hardening, and he touched my hair. "It's greasy. Have you been sweating?"

"Yeah, I took a long walk . . ."

"You look strung out. Has something happened?"

"Just feeling the time pressure."

He studied me, sniffing me out like a big fucking bear. I was cracking, fear and panic leaking from my pores.

"I better check on Anaïs," I mumbled, and I darted away.

She was sitting on the edge of the deck, legs in the water, and instinctively I knew I needed to touch her. Carefully, I rested my hands on her shoulders and began to gently massage her muscles. She let out a long exhale. I rubbed her neck and scalp, and it gradually calmed us both down.

"You always know how to ground me . . ." she said, swiveling around and kissing me in that last-night-on-earth way, and in spite of everything, I was able to get lost with her for a few minutes, a testament to the passion we still shared for each other.

But she could be in on the whole scheme, I warned myself. You have to find a way to let go and care only about finishing the double portrait.

"Bernard won't pay me for another week or two," I told her, "and he doesn't seem willing to give me an advance, so I won't have the money to ship the portraits, much less get a ticket to L.A."

"Are you finished with the last one yet?"

"Soon . . ."

"Why are you keeping it such a secret?"

"That's just the nature of it, I guess. It's between me and the image."

"When I watched you draw me yesterday, doing the Schieles, it scared me."

"It was that bad?" I smiled.

"No, no. It was like you'd moved beyond anything I could give you. The way you drew, with such vengeance, something violent and brutal in your face, your hands, like you'd kill whoever got in your way. And the intense beauty of the images, it was on another level."

The flame in her eyes and the tone of her voice seemed so heartfelt, and I wondered what would happen to her—her studies, her career—if her uncle and father went to jail.

"When are you doing your presentation?" I asked.

"There's an opening in three days that I might take."

"I should be done by then. Maybe I'll come with you to Paris, see if I can ship off the pieces on credit or something."

"If not, I might have enough to cover it. I can try to borrow some money from Papa too."

"Thank you, Anaïs."

fifty-four

In the middle of the night I woke up with wild, racing thoughts. With Hal hovering around, everything could change in seconds, and there was no way to know how much time I had to finish the double portrait. I slipped out of bed, put on a jacket and jeans, and climbed barefoot to the fourth floor. Opening the trunk, I lifted out the spider drawing with Anaïs's lines roughed in, and also the drawings of Anaïs where I'd captured her expression just right. I went outside and put on my boots. Then I had to take them off and creep back to the kitchen to retrieve the flashlight.

The stall gate squeaked loudly and I cursed it. Ducking inside, I left the gate ajar and watched for any lights turning on inside the château. The recessed windows, raked with light from below, looked sinister. I shut the gate and trained the flashlight on the blank canvas.

Transposing the spider drawing onto the canvas was tricky in the stark spot of illumination. I miscalculated one of Sophie's arms and it fell off the canvas just past the elbow. I kept hearing noises and would rush to the gate and peek through the crack to see if someone was approaching. After two hours of this, a barrier of aggravation had built up between me and the image, and I was never able to delve in and get lost.

By dawn, I was completely drained and the double portrait was a mess of lines on the canvas. I can't work like this. What the hell am I going to do?

I peeked out the gate. Sunlight was tinting the sky. The entrance door was closed and no one stood in or passed by the windows. It was time to get back into bed with Anaïs and try to sleep.

fifty-five

When I entered the kitchen, Jean Luc was standing at the window. He turned and set his eyes on me.

"What were you doing in the stall?"

"Finishing the portrait you wanted me to do," I managed to say. "If Anaïs gets wind of it she'll go ballistic."

"Sophie didn't tell you?"

"Tell me what?"

"We decided against it."

"Well, you don't care if I do it anyway, do you? I have a show coming up and they need a third piece."

He shrugged. "Don't expect me to pay you."

"That's fine."

In the cool morning gloaming, his body looked wide and stout like a file cabinet, and I remembered his meaty palm and thick fingers stopping me in the upstairs studio.

"Where were you yesterday?" he asked me.

Don't swallow. Keep breathing.

"I went to the art-supply store in the morning," I said as casually as I could. "Um, then I took a walk. That's why I was late for lunch . . ."

"You act paranoid. Even Bernard asked me if something had happened between you and Anaïs. Like you're, I don't know, hiding something . . ."

I turned the panic into a yawn. "I have to get back to bed," I said, and I stepped away from him, got to the stairs, and didn't look back.

fifty-six

L ying in bed next to Anaïs, I stared at the ceiling. Cold shivers and
hot flashes traded blows. I needed to get away from them for a
day or two. Once I gathered myself, I could come back and finish the
double portrait.

Breakfast. I forced myself to eat. Didn't avoid Jean Luc's eye.
Held it together with an iron will. No mention of Anaïs's outburst.
A new tablecloth, plates, and glasses. Sophie fussed over the croissants. Jean Luc announced he was *taking the day off from tennis* and
planned to fix some things around the château. Was he keeping an
eye on me? It felt like a hive of bees in my stomach, nerves tingling,
and as soon as Anaïs finished her coffee, I took her outside.

"I think I need a day off," I confided. "Just to spend with you
somewhere. Can we go to your place in Paris?"

"Sure. I have to go back for my presentation anyway. We could
even leave today."

"Parfait," I said. "Let's get out of here."

fifty-seven

A naïs's apartment was in Le Marais and I recalled walking these same streets weeks ago with my skis on my shoulder, invisible to some, offensive to others, and very much resigned to my failure as an artist. We climbed a circular stairway to the fifth floor. The door was sticky and difficult to open. Anaïs went in first and I followed her through a tiny living space with scratched parquet floors and only a few pieces of furniture, all antiques in near ruin. There was a nook on the far side with a four-burner stove and a compact waist-high fridge. Parting strings of black beads hanging in a threshold, I stepped with her into a small room with a futon bed, a stack of textbooks, and another stack of novels. There was a huge oak armoire in the corner, a chest of drawers next to it, and a tiny table that held a computer. The one picture up on the wall was a framed Lucian Freud lithograph of a naked man on a metal frame bed with a greyhound dog beside him. The window in the bedroom looked out at other apartment windows and down into a brick courtyard.

"As you can see, I don't spend much time here," she said, dropping her bag. "Would you like some tea?"

I nodded, followed her out of the bedroom.

"Would it be possible for you to do renderings of the love nest for me?" she said. "It would really help my presentation."

"Of course."

"I'd like to do it tomorrow. The professor has an opening."

After rummaging some colored pencils from a drawer, I used the examples she'd sketched out on her iPad to make detailed drawings of the structure. Two hours later, I finished the last love-nest drawing and showed them to her when she stepped from the shower. She jumped up and down and kissed me all over.

Anaïs took me to a restaurant atop the Pompidou museum with spectacular views of Paris: an undulating landscape of rooftops, the Eiffel Tower jutting into the sky, the ivory dome of Montmartre glowing in the night. She was friends with the maître d' and he gave us a seat next to one of the big windows. She unwrapped her scarf with Paris like a halo behind her and for a moment I escaped everything that was threatening to tear us apart.

Then my curiosity, a sense of self-preservation, resumed its poking and nagging, and I couldn't push away the need to know any longer.

"Does Bernard sell a lot of fakes?" I asked while unbuttoning my jacket.

"Not that I know of," she said nonchalantly. "Are you regretting doing them?"

I shrugged, watching her reaction very closely. "What about stolen stuff?"

"Stolen? Where did you get that idea?"

"I don't know. It's not that different, is it?"

"Of course it is," she insisted.

I gave her as vague a doubtful look as I could.

"You see," her voice rose, filling with ardor, "passing off fakes is a kind of poetic justice, a way to get even with all the pompous dealers and critics he's been at the losing end of. Think about it. Once your Schieles hit the market, the same critics and buyers that discounted you will be drooling over them."

Hearing her articulate it like that filled me with a kind of music, the music of sweet redemption. I recalled drawing the fakes, the lines coming from somewhere beyond what we could see or comprehend, out of thin air, like I was tapped into a pure source of creativity and it was running through my veins. It was so beautiful and fulfilling that I hadn't needed food or sex, nothing, nothing but the visceral charge of making a sublime image. And to envision my work fetching the respect of big collectors, not to mention their big money, washed me with a kind of high that felt healing.

"You understand," she said, beaming.

"Oh yeah, I totally get it."

She gave me one of her intoxicating smiles and I told myself that it made sense, fit her personality, to simply enjoy fooling the gate-keepers, as I did, and by producing fake Schieles, not selling stolen ones, she wanted us to make enough money so we could chase our dreams, the very dreams those gatekeepers were blocking.

After dinner we went to her friend's apartment and borrowed two bikes. As we peddled through the back streets of the city, Anaïs introduced, what was for me, a secret Paris: a series of canals and waterways, tributaries of the Seine, that jigsawed through the city. My favorite part was waving to the quirky people who lived in their boats, lanterns hanging off a mast, something from a bygone Paris whose mere existence enchanted me.

We ended up on the back side of La République, along Canal Saint-Martin. It was quaint and narrow, lined with trees growing from the wide flagstone walkways that hemmed in the water, cross-hatched with bridges, some steel, industrial-looking like an Erector Set. Anaïs sang Serge Gainsbourg songs while we dangled our feet over one of the bridges.

fifty-eight

In the morning, I walked with her to the Sorbonne and wished her luck and then went to Café de Flore, where we'd gone the day we met. The headlines of the *International New York Times* were all about a terrorist attack in Switzerland and the tightening of the border, but I noted a short related article about a man being caught in the terrorist dragnet trying to smuggle a stolen Picasso across the border.

Wonder if Hal had anything to do with that?

I ate eggs with bacon and waited for the gallery that Janet had a relationship with to open. In a few days, I anticipated, I'll be finished with the double portrait, ship them all off, and then once Bernard pays me I can get on an airplane, hopefully with Anaïs, and go to L.A.

"Mind if I join your table?" came a voice as Hal appeared at my side.

It startled me and after the initial jolt, I just stared at my newspaper.

He sat down. "Anything to report?" He pointed at something in the paper that was facing him.

"No. We had to come back for her school presentation," I said, hiding behind the paper.

"Hand me a section so it looks like that's what we're talking about."

I handed him the business section.

"Well, Nathan, you're either with us or you're against us. What is it?"

"I haven't seen any Schieles."

The waiter came and Hal ordered a coffee. He looked over the paper and didn't say anything to me, which was an effective way to apply pressure. When the coffee came Hal started counting his money on the table, the confused tourist. Then he slid a five-euro note to the middle of the table.

"There's a phone card under the note," he said. "Once it's in your phone, and your phone is on, it will allow us to listen to any nearby conversations. Just in case."

I lowered the paper. "Just in case what?"

"In case you talk to Bernard or Jean Luc about the Schieles."

I shook my head and used his annoying relentlessness to help me project insolence.

"Hey," he said. "Maybe you like Bernard. Maybe you don't want to hurt Anaïs. I get it. But the one they work for, the mastermind, he's a very bad man."

I opened my hands.

Hal continued. "Last year, he sold a Picasso and a Degas—seminal works that had been looted by the Nazis—to a Saudi prince. Before he does any more damage, we want to find him. We know he's a Swiss citizen but that's all we've got on him."

Hal put his hand on my shoulder and I scowled at him and he removed it.

"The Jewish families who had their art stolen want to find him. As an artist, as a decent human being, you should want those paintings in museums for all the world to enjoy, not locked away in some Saudi prince's lair. It's immoral."

"I agree," I told him. "But what does that have to do with the Schieles you're after?"

"Whoever has the Schieles will most likely fence them through the Swiss guy. There are four other people we suspect might have them, all of whom work with this guy, but I don't have enough re-sources to tail everyone."

"Okay," I said. "I'll keep an eye out and let you know."

He watched me for a moment. "It's the right thing to do," he said, and then he took his time finishing his coffee before dropping the newspaper on the table and leaving.

fifty-nine

I had no choice; I would have to tell Hal the truth. Where before I'd noodled with the idea of taking the path of least resistance— finish the double portrait; borrow enough money from Anaïs to at least ship the portraits, or finagle a way to ship them on credit; and then worry about my plane ticket, letting Bernard and Hal fend for themselves—now I had a larger moral obligation to help nail the Swiss scoundrel and the Saudi prince. Abruptly the clock was ticking, accelerating time, and it galvanized the urgency to finish the double portrait.

But waiting a few days to call him wouldn't matter. That's all I needed in order to get it done. The problem was I had to get back to the château, the canvas, and find a way to work on it without Anaïs knowing.

"Shit," I said aloud, causing the nearby patrons to turn and glare at me.

I walked out of the Flore and found the gallery a few blocks away. I introduced myself and inquired about shipping the pieces on credit. "Impossible," was the manager's response. It would cost around eight hundred euros. I had thirty-five in my pocket. I hoped Anaïs would come through.

She had given me the key to her place. Around noon, I returned to her apartment and waited for her. I was on edge, pacing around the small living room, and then the question of what would happen to Anaïs if her uncle and father were arrested crashed my thoughts again. Would she be arrested too? Tried as an accomplice?

Her landline rang. It was near the front door.

"How'd it go, baby?" I said into the phone.

"It's me."

I held the phone away from my ear.

"You're alone, no?" Sophie said. "I just spoke with Anaïs."

I brought the phone back to my ear. "Yes, I'm alone."

"Jean Luc is gone. We might only have twenty-four hours. If you come on the one-o'clock, I can get you from the platform. Bernard's coming now, must go . . ."

The phone went dead.

Before calling back, I needed to give her time to get free of Bernard. But I didn't have her number so I tried star 69, figuring she'd let it go to voicemail and hoping the number would be on her greeting. It didn't work, just dead air. Looking out the window, I tried to understand what she wanted. Was she going to help me finish a third piece for the L.A. show or did she still intend to seduce me, perhaps as a way to get back at her husband?

It doesn't matter, I argued, scrambling to find a piece of paper and a pencil. This is a lucky break that you won't get again. Hastily, I wrote Anaïs a note, using the excuse of *a bolt of inspiration* and leaving my cell number so that she could call to let me know how her presentation went. Then I took the metro to Gare de Lyon where I boarded the one-o'clock to Grez.

sixty

Measuring how much daylight was left, maybe three hours, I stepped off the train onto the platform. Sophie was behind the wheel of the Citroën. She'd borrowed it on some pretense, I assumed.

"Hi," I said when I got in the car.

"Ça va?" she said.

"Oui, et toi?"

She looked me up and down. "Oui," she said, and she accelerated, bouncing us along the dirt road through the rolling fields. We didn't talk. Driving with two hands on the wheel, she never even looked at me, weaving that circuitous route through the village. She dropped me at the gate and told me she'd be right back.

I went straight to the first stall and pulled out the canvas and easel. Lugging them along the drive and up the disjointed flight to the kitchen, I took a long tug from a bottle of red on the countertop before hauling them up to her studio.

Ten minutes later, I'd retrieved my materials and the crucial drawings and was setting up when she entered the room. She wore jeans, a sweater, and thick socks, and she sat on the floor with her back against the far wall. Her face was soft, arms lithe, an aura of submission—something that had always been missing in our sessions.

I positioned the canvas on the easel faced away from her, cognizant of how she might react once she got a good look at the double portrait—it could go either way—and I hoped to delay her response for as long as possible.

"Please take the spider pose," I said.

She slipped off her clothes, laced her ballet slippers, and gathered herself into the pose, arms dangling between her wide-set knees. From the very first line, much like when I'd made the Schieles, the light met her body and formed shapes of their own accord, burning the atmosphere, captured instantly as if I were merely snatching them out of the air. Sophie shifted, stretched, curled with each of my requests; otherwise the only sounds were her grunts and groans. Two bunches of sinew, flexing from each gluteus, turned out to be a vital new detail that made her strength more palpable without having to cheat reality.

Within an hour, the interplay of lines formed a being half creature, half woman, part mother, part vixen, hovering over a faintly sketched-in Anaïs, whom the spider mother both loved and feared.

"I need a break," Sophie said, severing the flow.

"Of course."

She lifted out of the pose and walked into the bathroom, shutting the door. A grainy blue light filled the windows. I laid the good Anaïs studies on the floor at the foot of the easel. Miraculously, two of them fit right in, only the slightest rescaling required, and I drew the lines easily. Anaïs's expressions were so vibrant, coalescing in a flurry of deep slashes, that I might not need her to pose again.

I opened the tin of paints, found my favorite brush, and applied the gouache. With each brushstroke a charge seemed to break free. From one dab to the next, the image bleeding through the stains appeared to step further and further beyond its two-dimensional confines and spoke to me, in Anaïs's eyes, mouth, rested cheek, curled body. When I used a thicker brush over the spider, she began gathering the light, as if siphoning it from her daughter, and I wanted to take it right up to the edge. When something told me to stop, I pulled back and closed my eyes for a few seconds. Opening them, I saw the two women living and breathing on the canvas.

I heard Sophie pad from the bathroom. The light was dissipating and I dragged the canvas under the westernmost window, where the last vestiges of dusk filtered in. I used a very thin brush to add a dash of pale orange in Sophie's eyes then stepped back. The spider mother, with all her color and fully realized lines, overwhelmed the relatively unadorned girl cradling her foot.

"What do you think?" I asked, swiveling the easel around so that she could view the painting—for the first time.

Her eyes narrowed, scanning the image, body rising and falling with her increasingly rapid breathing. She turned away, searching the room as if for a familiar chair or photograph. Her eyelids closed, brows lifting against the skin, holding there with a deep breath, and then opened, a bewildered look directed at me.

Could she really be so surprised?

She seemed to read the question in my face. "I've always been tangled up inside my relationship with Anaïs . . ." Her eyes drifted onto the canvas. "I've never stood outside myself and seen what it looks like, between us . . ."

Her head tilted away from the canvas, as if she'd been slapped by a scolding hand. She looked sorrowful, maybe even horrified.

"That's all you see?" I asked.

She dared to glimpse it again, over her shoulder.

"The mother is torn . . . afraid of being cast aside . . ." she said.

"And the girl?"

She closed her eyes. "A hint of admiration for the mother . . ."

"Yes . . ."

"It's astonishing . . ." she said with her eyes closed.

I stepped around to the front of the canvas, levitating from the knowledge that I'd really done it. Finally gone where I'd needed to go. It was tangible evidence that my dubious choices had been justified, were even necessary—simply the price of making art.

In my periphery, Sophie took an unhurried step closer to me, strands of hair falling across her face. "Am I really so ruthless?" she said coyly, moving in until her nipples pressed against my arm.

"Remember what you said about guilt?" I told her.

It made her chuckle and she smiled at me, a peace between us, and I reached for the canvas; it needed to dry in the stall before I brought it to Paris and shipped it off with the others, after which I'd call Hal. At that moment, smooth, delicate fingers curled around my wrist and guided my hand behind me. I felt the dew of dried sweat as my fingertips traced her inner thigh.

"Isn't this what you want?" she said, directing my hand upward.

A tiny balloon of heat grazed my fingers before I felt her sex. She was reclaiming the advantage and I told myself to get away.

"He always asks if you tried to touch me," she whispered at my nape. "Now I don't have to lie."

My fingers slipped inside her. I was on the cusp of no return, hunger gathering, blood draining from my head. I searched for the door, found it, and walked out.

At the river, I stripped down and dove off the barricade, and the cold water took all my breath away.

sixty-one

I floated on my back to the levee, energized by the belief that the double portrait was the best work I'd ever done. Out of the corner of my eye, I spotted two beams in the night, then saw the Citroën parked in the drive, headlights still on, and I felt my ebullience waning.

I got out of the water and collected my clothes from the lawn, wrapped myself in a towel, and went inside. Reaching the landing, I was met by Bernard, Jean Luc, and Anaïs standing in the kitchen. Sophie was pouring four cups of tea, cool as a cucumber, leaving me to face their scrutiny without any buffer.

Anaïs touched two fingers to her neck, and her angry stare flinched toward her mother before settling back onto me. I hope Sophie hid the canvas, I thought, and I strode right up to Anaïs, kissing her unresponsive mouth.

"Bolt of inspiration, huh?" she said.

I nodded demonstratively. "It's been going really well."

"I see," she said, glancing toward her mother. "Let's have a look."

"It's not ready for criticism. I still need to feel alone with it. Give me another day or two."

Jean Luc's eyes had been boring into me and I refused to look at him. Being nude beneath the towel wasn't helping the situation, and I took Anaïs's hand and led her toward the stairs.

"Come with me," I said.

She resisted, tugging behind me. At the stairs I let go of her hand.

"What's wrong?"

"How come you didn't call to let me know Papa had left?"

"Didn't notice. I was busy working."

Jean Luc, Bernard, and Sophie were watching from the kitchen.

"I don't believe you," Anaïs said.

"How am I supposed to know where your parents are? What does it matter, anyway?"

"Because you know that Maman is desperate for attention."

Sophie huffed. "Ooh la la. Don't drag me into your lover's quarrel."

Jean Luc turned and studied Sophie, quietly assessing her reaction. Was he prying for evidence that she'd taken the game too far, or was he getting off on the idea?

"But your father's here," I said. "I don't understand why you're upset."

"Don't play dumb."

"Honestly, Anaïs, I'm totally confused."

Bernard intervened. "He's been working, not chasing after your mother, Anaïs. You've let your imagination run away."

Sophie pursed her lips and nodded. Jean Luc still had his eyes on his wife and he suddenly barked, "Enough. Let's have a drink and start the dinner."

I grabbed Anaïs's hand and led her to the bedroom.

sixty-two

I rubbed her shoulders and head and she had finally calmed down when Jean Luc called from the top of the stairs. He wanted her to help with the dinner. She slid off the bed and pecked me on the cheek. "I have to," she said, tucking into tight jeans and a blouse before hastening out the door.

I waited a few seconds and then went upstairs to check on the canvas and figure out where to hide it. Anaïs still didn't know that her mother was part of the portrait and revealing that now would be quintessentially bad timing. I also needed to choose a few sketches to justify my *bolt of inspiration* in case she insisted on seeing something.

The canvas wasn't in the studio, only the easel, and it wasn't anywhere I looked on the fourth floor. Had Sophie confiscated it, the shame too much to ever face again? Once more, I had to acknowledge that she could effectively destroy the double portrait with one word to Anaïs. I rushed, as quietly as possible, down to the second floor. When I reached the landing, I could hear Jean Luc and Anaïs in the kitchen. I tiptoed along the hall to Sophie's bedroom. I knocked quietly and she opened the door.

"Where's the canvas?"

"In the stall."

"Thank you . . ." I took her hand, held it, trying to convey everything with the gesture, even pleading for her to stay on my side. "Are you coming down?"

"Why? They only want each other. Not us. I'm tired of always having to serve him," she went on. "Look at how crazy it makes our lives."

Nodding sympathetically, I felt that ripple of anxiety again. The web ran wide and deep; all alliances were tenuous, easily swayed from one look or comment to the next. Who knew how long ours would hold?

"I better go down there so she doesn't get suspicious," I said, forcing myself to kiss her cheek, before attending to Anaïs, my lover and primary concern.

sixty-three

Jean Luc was opening a second bottle of wine when I entered the kitchen. Anaïs was reporting on her presentation to him and Bernard, which I realized I'd forgotten to ask about. Listening, I learned that she'd received a high mark and that the professor was going to recommend her for the coveted internship at a respected engineering firm in Paris.

"Bravo. This calls for champagne," Jean Luc cheered. "But we have none so I'll open a bottle of the best whiskey."

He rummaged in the pantry, the sound of another—perhaps hidden—compartment opening and then closing, and returned with a pint of whiskey. He poured four shots and handed them to us and we all clinked.

Bernard gulped his down and said he had to go. He glanced at his brother and pointed at his wristwatch, and Jean Luc nodded. What was that about? I wondered. Then Bernard kissed Anaïs and congratulated her again. I walked with him to the landing and was about to mention the money when he said, "I've got good news. Come by in the morning and we'll settle up."

"Parfait," I said, and I thanked him, and as he went out the entrance door, Sophie descended into the kitchen.

By the time dinner was served, we'd drunk the second bottle of wine and half the whiskey. Sophie and Jean Luc were quite drunk. The steak was overcooked and the sautéed vegetables were limp. Jean Luc asked the women if they liked the food and they gushed with compliments. When he criticized the steak, they argued that he was better than any chef in France. Jean Luc turned to Anaïs, said something about a new tennis racket he'd tried, and Sophie rolled her eyes, cheeks and mouth rigid, and I saw a shadow of hatred in her face that gave me the chills.

"I'll be gone tomorrow," Jean Luc announced, "but when I get back I'm going to take my girls for a big fall shopping spree in Paris. No limits. Anything you want."

Sophie looked over at me and tilted her head toward Jean Luc, letting her face fall, eyelids droop—he's such a blowhard—and in my periphery, I saw Jean Luc watching our exchange. Feigning that I hadn't noticed Sophie's look, I deftly cast my eyes at Anaïs. She was describing some shops she wanted to go to, and from the corner of my eye, I saw Jean Luc turn and stare bitterly at his plate of half-eaten meat.

"It's not enough to have my daughter," he muttered, teeth gnashing.

I pretended not to hear him, hoping he'd blown off some steam and, drunk, would move on to something else.

"You want it all," he said, eyes finding me across the table.

Again I pretended not to hear him, forcing my attention on Anaïs, who was telling her mother about a shop called Chloé.

"You want my wife and my daughter for your paintings," he said loudly, and Anaïs stopped talking. "They would make you famous."

I gave him a look of confusion. "I think Anaïs has taken care of that. They love her portraits back home."

"Why don't you show us what you've been working on?"

"Like I said, it's not quite ready."

He looked at Anaïs and said, "He's doing a portrait of Maman."

Anaïs's face turned to plaster. White and lifeless. The tangled web of deception was about to unravel. I had to put a spin on it.

"Oh, you mean the portrait of Sophie you've been nagging me to do?"

"Boof," he groused. "You've been drawing her naked for weeks behind Anaïs's back."

"And you've been offering me money to do it, threatening to throw me out if I didn't."

"Don't deny it, Jean Luc," Sophie cut in. "You've been pressuring me too."

"Putain," he barked at her, enraged by her corroboration, and he picked up his glass and sloshed his wine at her. It missed and landed on the table. "You lust after him right in front of me. You meet with him in secret. You call him to the château when I'm gone."

"No, Jean Luc," she retaliated. "You ask me to do these things so you won't be impotent." She looked at Anaïs. "It stimulates him. I'm his wife so I'm obligated to make him feel like a man, no? But I've only gone as far as flirting."

"Bullshit," he said, standing, banging the table with his legs. "I'm going to find the drawings you flaunted at me."

Fearing he knew where they were and that he would bring down the nudes, I jumped in: "But that was the deal we made so you wouldn't kick me out," I said. "I would only do a few drawings for you, that was all."

"I want to see them," Anaïs said, and we all turned and looked at her.

Everything slowed down. I slipped inside a cocoon, where preserving the canvas was the only thing that mattered. I would do or say anything to protect it.

"I'll go get them," I said.

With a steady hand, I plucked five drawings of Sophie, no longer needed, from the old trunk and then gathered the remaining ones, the nudes, and hid them on a perch outside the bathroom window, to one side, out of view. I'd discard them later, throw them in the river, burn them.

When I returned to the kitchen, Jean Luc was standing, unsteadily, with his hands on his hips, a severe expression on his face. Anaïs was chewing her fingernails. Sophie was sitting in her chair, her pointer finger sliding back and forth along the inside of her necklace.

"Here they are," I said, and I laid them on the table, stepping back to give her space.

Apprehensively, Anaïs approached. The top one depicted Sophie in the second position, feet turned out, heels shoulder-distance apart. Anaïs pushed that one aside and studied the next sketch and then the next. They were innocent enough but her eyes slashed across the room, landing on me. She shook her head.

"Anaïs," I implored. "They . . ."

I felt Sophie's knifing gaze and glanced at her. She dipped her head toward Jean Luc: focus the blame on him; he deserves it.

"They were for your father. You know there's no denying him. I had to do it or he said he'd kick me out."

"It's true," Sophie said. "He threatened both of us. He'd take a lover if I didn't turn him on." She thrust her chin at the drawings. "This turns him on."

"They're lying to cover up their affair," Jean Luc asserted. "Where are the nudes?"

I shook my head. "That's bullshit," I told him. "You know I never made any nudes."

Jean Luc charged at me and I stepped aside. He went stumbling into the far wall. He turned, caught his breath, and pointed his finger at me.

"You're a fucking cancer. I forbid you to be in my house. Leave now."

"If he leaves," Anaïs spoke up, "then I leave too, Papa. You're drunk and it's not his fault that your little game with Maman has gotten out of control. He's desperately trying to make it as an artist and you used that against him."

His face was red, almost comical, but for the fact that he looked like he wanted to tear me to pieces with his big hands. Then he glanced at Sophie.

"You're a fucking whore," he said, and he pushed off the wall and stomped across the kitchen. He got to the landing and his heavy body thudded down the steps, then the creak and bang of the door. The three of us didn't move, each frozen in place.

"You were all sneaking around behind my back," Anaïs finally broke the stalemate.

"But I really had no choice," Sophie said.

"Of course you had a choice."

They studied each other.

"Oui," Sophie acquiesced. "I was trying to keep the family together. That was what I chose."

Anaïs's brow lowered and her mouth parted. But she didn't speak and her reaction was inconclusive. The moment seemed to hang in suspension.

"Did he encourage you to flirt with Henri, too?" she said after a few beats.

Sophie cast her eyes away with shame, nodding. "It's hard to explain, Anaïs, what goes on between a man and a woman after so many years of marriage. We become so full of compromises."

"Did you sleep with him on the boat?"

"No. Nothing. I just asked questions and let him talk about himself."

"De rigueur."

"Oui, de rigueur."

Anaïs turned to me. "But sitting for someone is quite different, no?" she said, and then she returned to her mother for an answer.

Sophie made a dismissive gesture with her head.

I caught Sophie's eye. If you don't tell her, I will. Protecting the double portrait was one thing, but I couldn't lie to her any more. She'd stood up for me. I owed her the truth.

Just the thought of divulging our intimacy seemed to overwhelm Sophie and she closed her eyes.

"We did not sleep together," Sophie said with her lids shut. "But we touched."

Anaïs raised her arm and slapped her mother across the cheek, sending her wheeling out of the chair and onto the floor. I leapt between them and grabbed Anaïs's wrists. She thrashed her arms and kicked at my shins. Pulling her close, I smothered her in my embrace and she bit my shoulder. It took a vicious tug on her hair to pull her off me.

"It became insufferable," Sophie called up from her crumpled position on the floor. "Jean Luc kept insisting that Nathan wanted me. It excited him to no end. But having to lie about it was too much, too humiliating. It was a matter of dignity."

I'd loosened my grip on Anaïs's hair and she was standing very still with her arms crossed. She watched her mother with a dumbfounded, openly gawking face, then shot me a strange, contemplative look and her eyes flashed with surprise.

Was she in the beginning stages of a nervous breakdown?

"Anaïs," I said to snap her out of it.

"It's not all just black," she said to no one in particular. "It hurts . . . but it's not killing me . . ."

"Okay," I said. "That's good. Let's sit down."

"Show me how you touched her."

"That's not going to help. We should take a walk, get some fresh air."

She ignored me and crouched down, eye-level with her mother.

"Show me, Maman," she whispered. "I don't want to have to always wonder. Please."

Sophie didn't hesitate. She got to her feet, one cheek bright pink with Anaïs's handprint, and approached me. I tried to step back and lost feeling in my body, going numb. She took my hand and slipped it down the front of her pants. With her palm over the back of my hand, she pushed my fingers inside her.

I didn't look at Anaïs. This was going too far—it would stain an indelible impression of us forever. I pulled my hand free and cast my eyes to the floor.

"Voilà," Anaïs sighed, and I turned.

The skin above her cheekbones and along her brow softened. Sophie was watching her with a wholly unguarded, defenseless expression that I'd never thought was possible in her. Anaïs stepped forward and hugged her mother. It was the first time I'd ever seen them embrace, other than the perfunctory greeting kiss on the cheek. No matter how dubious or perverse, I surmised, Anaïs had, at long last, gotten what she most wanted from her mother: evidence that she wasn't perfect, that she too was flawed and vulnerable.

They both began to cry in each other's arms, and it was clear that they'd been starving for this moment for a long time.

sixty-four

I went up to our room so they could be alone. Yes, I'd sacrificed everything for the double portrait, protected it like a baby, but now I wondered if it was worth it.

I put my face in my hands. I saw myself sitting alone in some apartment, the portrait up on the wall, even up on some big collector's wall, and there I was gazing at it, trying to squeeze some sort of affection, some sort of inspiration from it. But it was made of linen and paint, not flesh and blood. A single golden nugget, not the source, not the mother lode, and I couldn't picture fleeing the château and leaving Anaïs behind. She was part and parcel of how and why I made art now, my wellspring, and without her by my side I saw it all evaporate.

But, after tonight, the double portrait might be all I have left.

If she doesn't come up soon, I'll go downstairs and plead with her, bribe her, anything. If anyone would understand why I did what I did, it would be her.

Screaming. Echoing from below. I listened and walked out of the bedroom, following the sound of another voice. When I reached the landing, I heard Anaïs.

"Put it down, Papa."

I descended to the kitchen.

Jean Luc was holding an old, mottled pistol in Sophie's general direction, where she stood in the middle of the kitchen. Anaïs stood an equal distance from them, but not in the line of fire. As I came down into the kitchen, he trained the pistol toward me. I stopped on the last stair.

"You've turned them against me," he said, eyes bloodshot, fixing the pistol barrel on my chest—a small dark portal of death at the mere twinge of a finger.

"We're not against you, Papa," Anaïs pleaded.

"Jean Luc," Sophie said to him. "Anaïs and I thought our little misunderstanding was over." She looked to Anaïs.

"Yes, Papa. It's over now."

While Anaïs continued to try to convince her father that it was all behind them, Sophie shot me a pointed look, urging me toward action, then turned back to Jean Luc.

"We love and adore you," Sophie said with an angelic smile, but there were grooves of disdain along her upper lip and around her eyes. "Let's all go to bed now. You have to leave early in the morning."

He was distracted and I eased off the last stair, moving barefoot across the floor, focused on his bent arm holding the pistol. Sophie reached out for him with upturned palms like a figure in a Renaissance painting. That's when I burst into a sprint, crouching to tackle him, one arm chopping at his elbow like a football player trying to strip the ball. My shoulder planted into his ribs and I drove him into the pantry door. The wood split and I heard the pistol smack the floor.

I yelled for Sophie to pick it up. The impact had knocked the breath out of him and I used the opportunity to pin his arm behind his back, palming his head, pressing his face into the floor.

I glanced behind me. Anaïs was setting the pistol on the countertop. Jean Luc twisted and bucked, trying to free himself, so I clamped his arm further around his back. He groaned and gave up.

"He needs a good sobering up," Sophie called to me.

"Yes, he does," Anaïs added.

They were standing together as if cheering me on. I lifted him up, guided him down the rickety steps, and used his body to punch open the door.

sixty-five

I'd walk him to Bernard's and he'd take over from there.

"They call you Le Dildo, did you know that?" he sniggered.

"Really, Monsieur Limp Dick?"

"Be careful," he said in a grave, threatening voice.

"I'm not the one pointing guns at people," I responded, and he jammed his foot against my ankle, using all his weight, and tore free.

Immobilized for a moment, I shook out my leg and watched him stagger, zigzagging toward a horse stall— luckily not toward the one on the end with the canvas.

"You're a real pain in the ass," I sighed, and I trotted after him.

He threw open the stall doors and disappeared inside. I followed him in and heard a crack, steel on steel, like a big lock closing. Pivoting just in time, I ducked as a shotgun shell blew past me. I scrambled out and sprinted toward the entrance gate. He came out firing. A panel of the gate cracked apart in front of me. A lamp mounted to the side of the gate cast too much light and the gate would take too long to open.

I ran for the lawn, darker, and used the weeping willow to obscure myself. A limb burst to pieces above me and I got behind the trunk. He was shooting and stepping closer with each reload. The hanging limbs, skeletal and lifelike, were confusing him, so I stayed behind the trunk. I needed him to pass on one side or the other so that I could get behind him, or run.

He stopped moving, trying to wait me out, putting me at a disadvantage. I took off my jeans and got on my stomach and crawled toward the barrier. Lifting the jeans, I swung them high into the air, wafting them up and over the barrier and into the river, then snuck back toward the trunk.

He bit, shuffling quickly toward the river, shotgun at the ready. While he searched the water, I crawled up behind him. Three feet away, I exploded off the ground and slammed into his back. He fell onto the barrier, the shotgun discharged, and he bounced and rolled and then plunked into the river.

I heard splashing and looked for him but the water was black and then the splashing subsided. He'd swum to the far side. Would probably go down to the levee or beaver dam, cross, and come after me again.

"Thank you," I heard Sophie's voice, huskier than ever, behind me.

I turned and she stood on the lawn, a damsel-in-distress wax to her eyes, the mottled pistol dangling loosely in her hand.

"Let's hope that fucking shotgun is jammed," I said. "Maybe we should get the hell out of here."

"He's not coming back."

"I doubt that."

"He can't swim."

"What?"

Her eyes were big and wild, and she nodded, tossing the pistol into the river.

I swung my head over the water, moved along the barrier to where a slant of light from the house grazed the levee. My jeans were tugging back and forth at the apex of the levee, snagged by something, unable to take the ride over the fall. No Jean Luc though.

I dove in and traced the submerged portion of the levee all the way across the river. Nothing. I scoured the river floor a few feet away, the current carrying me into the levee twice. Nothing but silt and rock. Surfacing, shivering from the cold, I tore my jeans free of a lodged stick, oared my way back to the barrier, and pulled myself out of the water.

Sophie's intensity had eased. "As far as we know," she said breathlessly, "Jean Luc left, walked toward Bernard's."

Head ringing, I blinked—she was concocting an alibi for me. Not wanting it to be true, I took off and searched downstream. As I moved further down the river, it got darker and the water blended with the night. I stopped to let my eyes adjust.

"Jean Luc," I called.

"It's okay," Sophie's voice answered, startling me.

She appeared from the dark, moved closer, her breath warm against my cheek, sour, and then she kissed me on the mouth. A reward.

"He could've killed me," I told her. "It was self-defense."

"Your secret is safe with me," she whispered.

I saw myself in handcuffs, in front of a judge, then in a jail cell. My limbs turned to straw as I relented toward the inevitable: he was dead and she'd seen me push him into the river.

"Let's go inside," she said, taking my hand.

sixty-six

Anaïs was in her mother's bed, under the covers, waiting, when Sophie led me into the room. I glanced at the window facing the river. It provided a view of the entire scene between Jean Luc and me, albeit shrouded in darkness and obscured by the sprawling willow.

"Was he shooting at you?" Anaïs said, sitting up.

I nodded.

"Where is he now?"

I deferred to Sophie. "He must've gone back to Bernard's," she said. "Hopefully he ran out of bullets."

Anaïs got out from under the covers and kissed me.

"You saved us, mon amour," she whispered in the same breathless way her mother had.

I couldn't get my bearing, the room seemed off-kilter, and my mind spun, roving the deep verses of the riddle. Over Anaïs's shoulder I saw Sophie watching us and I wondered if she was happy to be rid of him.

"You must be in shock," Anaïs said, resting her palm on my cheek.

I nodded. "I have to rest . . ."

"I'll come with you," she said, and she trailed me out the door.

With no memory of climbing the stairs, I eased onto the bed and she curled up against me.

"You really are my shepherd in the storm," she whispered.

Even in such bleak circumstances, the irony was not lost on me.

My betrayal, its revelation, had provoked the confrontation in which I'd protected her from her father, and which ended up convincing her that I was her shepherd in the storm.

Soon she was asleep, head on my chest, and night's dark voids pressed in from all sides. I'd contributed to her father's death. How would I ever make that up to her? Like a stranglehold around my neck, I felt infinitely, even obscenely, indebted to her. While at the same time, I worried about what would happen when the body was discovered. If Sophie held to her story, they'd think he fell into the river on the way to Bernard's and drowned. Could I really count on her?

Easing out from under Anaïs, I went to the back window and peeked down. Beyond the trickle of ambient light, the river was a depthless plane of ink. Where was his body? Ten miles down the river? Or stuck on the bottom somewhere? I raised my gaze. The forest was a void of blackness, silent, reminding me that I was on my own, with no one to turn to, not really.

I had to get the hell out of France, Europe, before anyone found his body. It could happen at any moment. Suddenly the knock at the door, the police, the questions—my living in the house, the nudes of mother and daughter, none of it would look good.

Should I leave right now? Start walking toward the train?

I crawled back into bed and wrapped my arms around Anaïs. Rising from a deep slumber, she kissed my mouth. "Je t'aime," she murmured, and she tumbled back to sleep.

sixty-seven

A bird chirping. Another bird singing an answer. I must have dozed off. I opened my eyes. Sunlight in the windows, a new day. With time to cull through a vast surplus of narratives and forge a comfortable distance, my unconscious had done its job and rationalized the whole fiasco. There was no reason to lose everything because a jealous, drunk Frenchman tried to kill me and I'd defended myself. That was unacceptable. I'd fought too hard for too long to sacrifice my triumph. I couldn't bring her father back; all I could do now was be there for her and try to make something out of all our hard work.

Every second counted. I had to put the blinders on and take action. First and foremost, secure enough money to send off the portraits and get us on the first plane to L.A. If pressed, Anaïs could surely scrounge up a few thousand euros—put it on a credit card—and once I was safely back in the states, out of the jurisdiction of the French police, it would be a lot easier to comfort her, give her my undivided attention.

I got out of bed, put on my damp jeans, and went to make sure he wasn't floating out in the open somewhere. If so, I'd hide him, buying us time to get out.

Nothing on the levee. I moved downstream, following the bank. Nothing along the muddy edges or in the shallows. I crossed the beaver dam and worked my way along the far bank. Maybe he did make it out of the river, I entertained, eyes sweeping more languidly over the water. Maybe he's asleep at Bernard's and soon I'll collect the money, at least enough to ship the portraits.

In a crook on the far side, a heap of debris broke the surface. I watched it move. It was trapped in a tight swirl of current, unable to swing free and join the main thrust of the river. It circulated closer to my side and I glimpsed his shirt and saw his back hunch out of the water, head submerged, legs dangling behind. He tried to kill me, I reminded myself, watching him go around for another turn.

I stopped breathing, went stiff and ice-cold. My legs were rooted in place and only my mind churned: the four of us trapped in the château, under the spell of desire, impelled to act dangerously. If only I'd walked away from her that first day in Paris or had left the château before her mother arrived, no one would be dead. What had compelled me to join in her parents' erotic secret and betray her trust? Why hadn't I been able to resist her uncle's illicit offer? It seemed to boil down to one basic impulse that we all shared: we were hell-bent, even destined, to avenge our underlying need to be loved.

"Got a plan?" a voice called, and I jerked back, tripping over some sticks.

I grabbed one of the sticks and got to my feet.

Hal waved at me from the far side. He was just upriver of the body, wearing a sweater and a cap, and I realized I was shivering.

"I'll meet you back at the dam," he said, and he started walking.

Would he draw a gun or just ask me, in that wholesome midwestern lilt, to take a ride with him? Would he turn me over to the French authorities or to the American Embassy? Nearing the dam, I glanced into the woods, leafless, the ground sodden. Turning, I caught a sliver of the château upriver. Then I crossed to his side.

"It was self-defense," I implored. "He shot at least five rounds at me. Apparently he can't swim."

"I know," he said. "One of my Toms heard the shots. Watched the whole thing through his infrareds."

"Then he'll vouch for me?"

Hal had grown a thin mustache and now it wrinkled when his mouth puckered. "Well . . ."

"Well what?"

"It would raise eyebrows," he said. "Know what I mean?"

"No, I don't. He's under surveillance, right? And your guy saw him try to kill me."

"The situation is complicated by the fact that he's a connected diplomat," Hal responded. "Even if we'd petitioned for a surveillance warrant, regardless of whether or not we got it, he would've surely been tipped off."

"So because the FBI isn't authorized to be watching him, you can't help me?"

Hal nodded.

"What the fuck am I supposed to do?"

"Tell me everything you know."

sixty-eight

After I'd laid out the whole ordeal—stolen Schieles and all—I had to sit down on a log and compose myself. When I looked up, Hal was rocking up and down on the balls of his feet, smirking with self-satisfaction.

"So what now?" I said.

"I got a sweeper tucking Blanchon's body away. You need to go back to the château and go through the motions until they make contact with you."

"I was thinking of just grabbing the portraits and splitting." I left out the part where Anaïs would come with me because I sensed he believed she was Bernard's accomplice.

"Come on now, Nathan."

"But I told you they have the Schieles. Why can't I split?"

"Because now we know that Jean Luc was the one that moved the merchandise across the border into Switzerland, using his diplomatic immunity. He was supposed to have taken the Schieles across early this morning. Now he's missing, so they're desperate. They need someone else to do it." Hal flashed that palsied smile.

"Then all you have to do is follow Bernard," I assured him.

"No. They want to use you."

"Me?"

After the terrorist attack in Zurich, Hal explained, the Swiss borders were on high alert and the risk of getting caught moving anything, much less stolen art, across the border had increased by a thousandfold. With Jean Luc missing, Bernard and his "associates" in Switzerland were scrambling for another way to get the Schieles to the Saudi prince in Bern. In their haste, they'd become a bit reckless and early this morning Hal had picked up cell phone chatter about the exchange, delayed twice already, and the prince getting impatient, threatening to scuttle the deal. Out of desperation, Bernard had introduced the idea of having me, based on my backcountry experience, ski the Schieles across the border.

"You're their last best chance," Hal said. "If they had to send a novice up there, the odds of him getting lost, falling into a crevasse, or triggering an avalanche would be too high. But not with you."

"Well, there's no guarantee. I've seen guides with twenty years of experience get taken out up there."

He blatantly ignored me. "And ironically," he continued, "it's a great plan. Except for the fact that we know about it, and we've got an inside man." Again, he flaunted that palsied smile, which I'd grown to despise.

"I'm not in good enough shape," I argued. "I'd have to train at altitude for weeks. And I only know certain routes. I'm not trekking across the fucking Alps on a route I don't know. That's a death trap."

"Don't worry, I got all that covered."

My scoff was more of a cough followed by a spit. I shook my head. No way.

"Or your other option is to face questioning by the French police about your involvement in the altercation that led to Jean Luc Blanchon's death."

My arms opened, mouth slightly agape, and I was shaking my head at him. He just stared back at me with those lifeless eyes.

sixty-nine

When I got to the house, Anaïs was in the kitchen, wrestling with the French press.

"Mon amour," she said, dropping the canister on the counter and rushing up to me.

Her hands cradled my face, those eyes still full of last night's devotion, the storm inside quieter than ever. I was pondering how I'd protect her from getting caught up in Hal's net when Bernard came up the stairs.

"Is Papa with you?" Anaïs asked him right away.

"No, my minnow. We think he took a late train to Paris. He had an early meeting today. You should have come for me last night."

"We thought he went back to your house," she told him. "I hope he's okay."

"Just a wooden mouth," he guffawed.

"It wasn't so funny last night, Bernard," she said.

"Mais oui," he said. "I need to take our Rembrandt away for a little bit. Okay?"

"Why?"

"I have an important errand to take care of, and since he's practically part of the family now, I thought, why not ask Nathan?"

"Hurry up," she said, clearly pleased. "I have my own personal errand for him . . ."

She winked at me and went upstairs.

When I turned, he was lighting a cigar at the dining table.

"I made Sophie show me the double portrait," he said, eyes gleaming. "It filled me with envy . . ."

Under the circumstances it was absurd, but I said, "Merci . . ."

"What will you call it?" he asked.

I glanced across the room and plucked the title from thin air. *"French Girl with Mother."*

He made a sound of garish satisfaction. And I expected questions about last night's incident with his brother, but he bypassed that.

"There's a complication," he said.

"What does that mean?"

"I can't get you the money quite yet. I'm sorry."

"Fuck," I told him, following Hal's script. "I need to ship the portraits by Thursday. Friday at the latest. This is my big chance, Bernard."

"I know, I'm sorry. I just need you to make a delivery for me."

"But can't you just give me a thousand euros right now?"

"There's nothing I can do. It's out of my hands."

I scuffed the floor with my foot, paced, and finally said, "Okay, what do I need to do?"

"Sit down and I will explain."

I lowered into a chair, felt the cell phone in my back pocket, and hoped I'd left it on.

seventy

Bernard asked me if I would be willing to climb high into the Alps, away from any resorts, *any eyes*, and transport the *real Schieles* hidden in my backpack to a Swiss border town.

"Why not just drive them across?" I challenged him, per Hal's instructions.

"Because the provenance of the drawings is in question," he explained. "A family grievance over inheritance. The authorities probably have someone watching me, so we have to do it another way. The Swiss border is infested with police looking for terrorists. I can't take a chance that we'll get searched somehow."

I acted as if that made me nervous, which wasn't difficult, and he told me he'd double my money to forty thousand euros.

"Fifty," I said, adamant.

"D'accord," he said.

I pretended to be impressed. He asked me if, based on my backcountry experiences, I knew a good route into Switzerland?

I feigned searching my mind, then told him I'd once skied a good route from St. Anton, Austria, to a Swiss village called Samnaun, which was true.

"Do you feel confident doing it alone?"

No, not really. "Sure," I said.

The drawings would be stored in metal tubes—two in each—and the enclosed ends would be further secured with tamper tape, he told me, unambiguously.

"Can you make the crossing in less than forty-eight hours?"

Anything less would push my slack conditioning past even the most optimistic expectations and would just be outright stupid, turning the already-dangerous trek into a suicide mission; but I couldn't take any longer than two days because the shipping deadline for the show was three days away, and I needed that third day to get back to the château and send off the portraits.

"Yeah," I said.

"Good, because I don't want them rolled up for longer than that."

He grabbed the whiskey bottle and poured two shots.

"Here's to your big show and the certain fame to follow."

We drank and shook hands.

"I'd like you to set out tonight," he said.

I nodded.

"I'll need your backpack to make the necessary preparations. Leave whatever ski gear you need in it."

I heard water running and Anaïs singing in the bathroom when I entered the bedroom. A leather suitcase was open on the floor, half-filled with some of the old sweaters and jackets I'd seen in the closet.

"Are you going somewhere?" I called into the bathroom.

"I thought we'd go back to Paris now that it's getting cold," she called over the gush of water. "Maman is going too; she expects Papa will return to their apartment after his meeting." Her mention of him made me cringe. "Believe it or not, those vintage coats are back in style. What's this errand he's got you doing?"

"He wants me to take some client he's wooing backcountry skiing," I said, repeating the story Bernard and I had settled on.

"This means he really likes you," she said.

Emptying my big backpack of everything but the essentials,

my mind looped round and round about what would happen if I got caught smuggling stolen Schieles into Switzerland. Would Hal really come to my aide, or would he let me take the hit? He hadn't specifically stated that the Swiss authorities were okay with his sting operation.

Absentmindedly, I was ripping gear out of the backpack and then restuffing it, until I forced myself to take deep breaths and come to terms with my predicament. The route out of St. Anton had a couple really dangerous sections, the glacier before the summit and the steep, avalanche-prone couloirs leading to the valley into Ischgl, a small village where I'd spend the night and recover, before making the border crossing. But on the other hand, I knew the route, a huge plus—except for the last leg into Switzerland because in order to avoid border patrol and ski patrol, who were on high alert, I couldn't take the ski trail across the border this time; I'd have to stay in the backcountry. Despite these hazards, it was better than the police holding me responsible for, and possibly finding me guilty of, Jean Luc's death.

I padded the sweat off my forehead with one of my flannels and then brought the backpack down to Bernard. He told me he'd be back in an hour.

seventy-one

The bathwater was no longer running when I returned to the bedroom.

"Mind if I put a couple things in your suitcase?" I said through the bathroom doorway.

"Whatever you want, mon amour . . ."

I carefully rolled the two Anaïs portraits into one of my flannels, and as I packed it between her sweaters in the suitcase, a terrible thought struck me. If something went wrong, I had no evidence of my grand achievement.

"I'll be right back . . ." I called, and hurried out of the house. Outside, I opened the stall doors. Light spilled onto the double portrait and I took a photo of it with my phone and quickly shut the doors. In the kitchen I had another whiskey and sent the photo to Janet.

Here's what I've been working on. Coming your way soon!

An hour and forty-five minutes later, Bernard dropped Anaïs and me at her apartment in Paris. The overnight train to St. Anton wouldn't leave for another six hours. Climbing the stairs, Anaïs was cheerful and talkative but I was distracted, unable to believe that I'd come out of this thing without losing her or the double portrait, maybe both. Even if I did somehow pull it off, how would I ever escape the stigma of playing a part in her father's death, ever shuck off its stench, regardless of the fact that he'd been shooting at me?

Hal had made it sound so simple. "Make the drop in Samnaun, return to the château to collect your money and your portraits, and then get the hell out of Dodge. The bust won't go down until after the Schieles are driven to the Swiss operative and he makes the exchange with the prince." Both of us had avoided the subject of Anaïs, what would become of her, as if we knew it was too flammable.

Hauling my backpack and skis up the narrow stairwell to her apartment, I flashed on the Saudi prince standing in his palace, gloating over his new collection of Schieles.

"Sacrificing four pornographic drawings to make sure that no more masterpieces are lost is a pretty good deal in my book," Hal had snapped at me earlier when I'd questioned his logic over forfeiting the Schieles.

It reinforced my theory about Hal: he didn't really care about the art; he was mostly in it for the bust.

Anaïs set down the suitcase and unlocked her apartment door. She pulled me through in a rush to make love, and we tripped over four big shopping bags.

"Oh, merde." She was laughing, holding on to me. "This was supposed to be your surprise. Before I saw your note and got suspicious."

I lifted the top item out of one of the bags. A fluffy white duvet.

"I want you to be comfortable here," she said, pulling out two feather pillows from the next bag, four thick bath towels from another, and showing me an assortment of men's toiletry products in the last.

"You're the sweetest," I said, and I helped carry the nesting things into her bedroom.

With her back to me, she dropped her bags and slowly took off her clothes. Untying her braid, she rested down on the futon, hair flowing out as if she were underwater. Her arms were at her sides like a girl on her wedding night waiting to be taken.

"I don't need to defend anymore," she said to me, as I stood over her. "I want to give you everything."

She pulled me down on top of her, her warm skin and greedy mouth melting all the wretched things closing in on us to sand. The grim circumstances flaked away under our frantic caresses, and we never let go, plowing deeper, tasting each other's salts, bleeding into one body, as if nothing could ever come between us, nothing.

In the aftermath, entangled, she said, "So, you really want to live with me?"

"Yes." I meant it with every fiber, even though I was about to put a dagger in our future.

"I want you so badly, Nathan," she said, and she wound herself around me tighter.

seventy-two

The train ride went on forever.

I could still feel the way Anaïs clung to me at the station, something I'd never felt from anyone, and now I hungered for it like an addict. Would I ever see her again? I beat the window with my fist until my knuckles bled.

Only hours ago, I'd been on top of the world, and then in one fell swoop, a little shove, it had all been ripped away, and now I was just hoping not to spend my life in prison.

I sat like a corpse until the train pulled into the Innsbruck station.

When I found the platform for my connection to St. Anton, I stretched out on a bench in the freezing Alpine air.

My cell phone buzzed and I sat up.

"Is that you loitering on the bench like a real ski bum?" asked Artur Dorfmein, a train conductor who lived in Feldkirch, and with whom I'd skied the backcountry of Liechtenstein last season.

"Yes, of course," I said, and we laughed, releasing some of the tension that had been seeping up my neck, shoulders, pinching my temples.

The train had just entered the station and I saw Artur wave from the engine car. He invited me to ride with him and a few seconds later I climbed in.

I told him about Anaïs, that I was moving in with her and that I was picking up some things I'd left in St. Anton—and in that moment, it all sounded plausible, a shadow life I'd probably never get to live. We got to talking about our Liechtenstein backcountry adventures and he mentioned the old World War II road that straddled the border between Liechtenstein and Austria. I'd forgotten about the road, but not the powder, and now recalled how we'd snuck back into Austria using that road after we skied down from the mountain, just to see if we could.

"The old guard tower made of logs," I said, "makes it feel like you're in the 1940s, you know?"

"Oh, yes," he said. "That road has a lot of history around it."

When the train pulled into St. Anton, I promised to look him up later in the season—we'd devour some fresh pulver—and I climbed out of the engine car.

seventy-three

I walked straight into the station bathroom, changed into my ski gear, and then crossed the town toward the Rendl side of the ski area, which wouldn't open for another few days, hoping I didn't run into anyone else I knew.

The town was quiet. Wooden chalets carved with edelweiss flowers, rosebuds, and snowflakes; cobblestone streets, smelling of tea and coffee and strudel. If only I could rewind time and lose my ambition and just be happy traversing the Alps, making some drawings, appreciating my freedom—something I feared might be gone forever now.

Before I knew it, I was pasting the mohair skins to the bottom of my skis, and then I started climbing the comeback trail toward the Moostal valley. Soon, jagged cliff faces appeared off my left shoulder and the mountain got steep. A gust of wind caught me by surprise and I slipped dangerously close to a sheer precipice.

Four hours later, the wind had died and the sun was high in the sky and I took a break at the Darmstädter Hut, a last remnant of civilization before I reached Ischgl.

After a sandwich and a bottle of water, I harnessed my pack, clicked into my bindings, and began blazing a trail toward the glacier above. Massive curving slopes of snow, shadowed by spires of rock. No movement but the drift of air funneling between the valleys, compressed in the gorges and couloirs, touching my face like Anaïs's fingertips when we made love.

Nearing the glacier, I saw cracks, dark veins, running up its gut, and the temperature had climbed too high for my liking, as the heat would burrow into those cracks and expand. Any extra weight might cause a chunk of glacier to break away, so I steered wide and chanced summiting the ridgetop via a flute of slippery vertical rock.

It was a bad choice, and now I'd gotten myself too far into its throat to turn back. Hugging the cold, ice-glazed jigsaw of rock, I even used my chin to gain purchase and inch upward, reaching blindly with one hand to find a hold. But it wasn't the fear of prison that drove me; it was wanting to crawl into a warm cozy bed with Anaïs, wake up with her in the morning, make love, eat breakfast, draw her, unravel something fascinating.

Crawling like a lizard out of the flute and onto the ridgetop, I dug my phone out of the pack. It had a signal. I called her but got voicemail.

"Hey, mon amour," I said, gazing at the Alps sprawling 360 degrees around me. "Just checking in. All is well. I wanted to hear your voice but . . . Je t'aime. Big kiss."

My quads were seizing up; I had to keep moving, and I edged into the couloir. It was full of light, forgiving powder, and I drifted away for a few minutes.

By sundown I made it to the pensione in Ischgl, buried among a smattering of chalets along a tight valley floor, far more provincial than St. Anton. Soothing my aching quads and buttocks in a hot bath, I called Anaïs at her apartment. Talking to her would keep my spirits buoyed.

I heard the click of someone picking up her landline; then it sounded like the phone was thrown and it banged on the ground and suddenly went dead.

I called back but there was no answer. So I called her cell. Again no answer. I left a message.

Famished, I went next door to the restaurant and ate a beef stew. When I got back to my room, I texted and then called Anaïs again. "Call me back, mon amour. Please."

Of course something was wrong, but in my stupor of exhaustion I couldn't cope with yet another hurdle, another test of will, and I decided not to worry. Before I got too tired, too bleary-eyed and absentminded, I had to focus on getting things rearranged. I opened my pack, unearthed the tamper tape I'd bought in Paris after Anaïs and I had made love, and then slid out the metal tubes with the precious Schieles inside them.

seventy-four

My phone was buzzing and it jarred me awake. I was still in my
clothes. On the floor. The room dark. The screen read a few
minutes after five a.m., and there was a text from a number I didn't
recognize, a video attachment. It might be new instructions from
Hal. I clicked on it.

A frozen image of a blonde woman. I pressed the arrow in the
center of the image.

The woman was three-quarters turned away from whoever was
shooting the video, presumably from his or her phone, as the image
came to life. She was posing like a ballerina, dressed in a tutu and ballet
slippers. When I got a good look at her in profile I recognized Anaïs,
wearing a blonde wig. She was clearly drunk, possibly high on something, and I could hear a party going on outside the dimly lit room.

"Come on, Jean Luc," Anaïs slurred in French, lifting her tutu,
naked underneath.

The camera moved in closer. Bile sluiced up my chest, burning
my throat, and I spit onto the floor.

"Nail me to the ground," she hissed, and I extended the phone
as far away from my face as possible, squinting as if at a horrific car
accident.

The camera went out of focus. Then it settled onto something,
knee-high, a chair, I guessed.

In the corner, I could make out a man's pants dropping around his ankles, and then he stepped forward and thrust upward, going completely out of frame.

Anaïs moaned. "Tell me what happened on the boat," she flirted.

"Nothing," came a less-husky, younger voice than I expected. "I gave her a lot to drink but she never reacted to any of my advances."

It sounded like Henri, and I was so relieved it wasn't her father that I thanked God aloud.

"Pretend I'm her," Anaïs coaxed. "Live out your fantasy."

No response. The grainy screen showed only the far wall, or perhaps it was a door. I could hear Henri sigh, searching for the right words.

"Jean Luc, you don't want me?"

"No, it's . . ." he finally responded. "Let's just be us."

"Ah, now you want me to be ashamed?"

"No, it's just a bit . . ."

"Deviant?" She scoffed and her voice, garbled by alcohol and spite, came through in bits and pieces. ". . . spend your life, even your sexual . . . in a petite bourgeois prison. Go find a little boring bitch . . . nose in the air."

I heard her pad across the room, heard a door open, and then light shot in, blowing out the screen. When the aperture adjusted, I could see a mass of bodies, the party I'd been listening to in the background, through the open door. Everyone was dressed up in costumes. Lots of white-robed emirs, Rastafarian wigs, and scantily clad Cleopatras. Then the video went black.

I flipped on the light. Moving to the window, parting the curtain, I looked onto the empty street. *I was showing him a real part of me . . . in bed . . . but he rejected it,* she'd told me cryptically when we'd first met in Paris, and now I understood what had happened.

But who sent the video? Henri, the jilted lover, was the obvious answer. It could be Sophie, though, or maybe even Hal. If so, what were they trying to tell me? I called the number to find out.

seventy-five

Every time I tried the number it went to an automated voicemail. It wasn't necessarily the content of the video that made me uneasy. I'd gotten used to, even become fascinated by, Anaïs's eccentric behavior and our uninhibited sex life—which had proved to be the impetus for great drawings. There was something else I couldn't put my finger on.

After restoring my provisions, I boarded the first ski tram out of Ischgl. Ischgl always opened a week or two earlier than St. Anton. There were only a few other skiers on it. One of them was a local guide who gave me a funny look and then ignored me—probably because he thought I was a good-for-nothing ski bum.

The next few hours were spent traversing cornices and climbing steep walls of rock and snow, weighted down with the questions that whoever sent the video obviously wanted to elicit.

If Anaïs knew, at least obliquely, about the sexual game between her parents, and took part in it by some measure, feeding off the threat of a paramour, like her father did, then what else was she hiding from me?

Had she invited me to the château not only as a way to challenge and provoke her mother, but also specifically as a resource for her and her uncle's forgery scheme—the legitimate *reproduction business* serving as the hook? In Paris, upon seeing my work, she would have easily recognized that I drew like Schiele, and she would've quickly deduced that I was a desperate artist—the perfect mark.

Repeated over and over, the questions eroded my strength and confidence and made the trek far more complicated than it already was. Shuffling along a narrow ridge on my skis, I stupidly closed my eyes to imagine her in the best possible light—waiting for me, soaking in a bath, biding her time at a café—and then I felt my skis slip on a patch of ice.

My eyes popped open and I was tumbling head over heels down the mountainside. I tried to jam a pole into the snow and the handle snapped back and punched me in the eye. Now I could see only one side of the slope, and as I tumbled I tried to turn my head to determine if there was rocks or a cliff in my pathway. The snow got deeper as I entered the heart of the slope and I twisted to get my skis sideways and dig in. Finally I skidded to a stop.

No broken bones and my pack was still strapped to my shoulders. Pressing snow against my eye for a few minutes to keep the swelling down, I then had to put the skins back on my skis and zigzag my way up the slope and onto the ridge. I could've been badly injured or even killed. Forget the video, what it might mean, and stay on task.

An hour later, I was again pondering our relationship, and at some point I realized that I'd hiked too far north. Now I had to backtrack the couloir I'd scaled and figure out another way around the rock massif. It would cost me at least an hour and a bundle of energy I wasn't sure I had.

As I descended the couloir, I entertained the idea that Anaïs would be gone when I returned to Paris, and that Bernard wouldn't be at the château, and I was convinced that I'd never see her again.

I stopped atop the Piz Rots at just over nine thousand feet and teetered at the edge of a huge cliff. Was I just being paranoid? Did the sender of the video intend to confuse me, keep me off-balance so that I wouldn't know who to trust? But why? Maybe it was to hurt my chances of making the delivery, as was now the case. But who would want that?

Abruptly the carousel of questions ground to a stop. I heard my stomach growl and realized it was completely empty and that I was dehydrated. When I reached into my pack for a bar, though, I couldn't stand the thought of food. I sucked water from the hydration bladder and sprayed it over my face in an attempt to think clearly. Cathedrals of white peaks went on forever. Otherwise nothing was clear.

The map indicated that from here I could dip down and cross into the Val Chamins via a mild slope face, and then into the Val Maisas, which would allow me to reach my final destination camouflaged by trees. I'd been traversing the highest, most shielded terrain in order to avoid detection from ski or border patrol.

As I crested the sidewall of the first valley, a voice called out from behind me. I turned and it was a border patroller on skis. He waved me down to where he stood, tucked on the side of the valley wall. He was a good ten-minute haul from me, I determined, and the ridge was all cliffs except at the top. I'd have to keep skinning upward for another twenty or thirty minutes to enter the next valley. Meanwhile, he'd simply enter from below and be ahead of me.

Gathering speed, I polled through the snow along the ridgeline and then launched off the cornice. Sailing over the cliff faces, the backpack drew my weight onto my heels. I rotated my arms, rolling up the windows, in an attempt to shift my weight forward. Twenty feet was not enough to regain my balance and when I landed the tails of my skis hit the snow first. For some reason, one ski didn't pierce the snow and my leg ricocheted into the air, hyperextending that knee.

A moment later, lying prone as if in a bathtub, I brushed enough snow off my face to finally breathe and a needle of pain gouged my knee. It would be a bitch to slog through the deep snow with a bum knee, especially now that I had to move fast.

Halfway across the valley, with still no sign of the patroller, I was in such paralyzing pain that I stopped and stuffed my ski pants with cold snow. It took five valuable minutes before my knee was numb enough to carry on.

It got me to the far side, only to hear the patroller call out. He was about a hundred yards below, shuffling toward me at an upward angle. If I didn't move faster, he'd cut me off before I got up and over the valley wall, where the forest would hide me.

I bit down on the hydration tube, chomping on it more as a way to eat up the agony than for the water. I lurched up the wall. When I looked back, he was about fifty feet away and I felt my body give out. The air seemed too thin, no longer filling up my lungs, and the more I gasped for oxygen, the more fuel I expended, a vicious cycle. Looking back to check on the patroller's progress again was out of the question and I had to fight the surreal desire to just plop down in the snow and sleep. The white, smooth contours seemed to bounce clipped, echoed voices at me. Will I go to jail for my sins? Is this the true price of making art? Anaïs will be drinking champagne in Corsica while I'm sleeping on a cement floor. I was a fool, a dreamer, all the more ridiculous because after proving the naysayers wrong I'd managed to sabotage my redemption.

I tipped forward, expecting to collapse in the snow, before I realized that I'd staggered up and over the sidewall of the valley and was now careening down the backside toward a cluster of trees.

Dodging them, shards of pain rippled from my knee to my hip, up my ribs, and all the way into my armpit. It was keeping me alert and I fed off it.

When I came through the first cluster and into a short clearing, my body tensed with the anticipation of the patroller leaping out and tackling me. The next hundred yards was like taking blind curves on a single-lane road, braced for a head-on collision at any moment.

It never came, but the anticipation severed my last nerve, and I was a bedraggled, starving, pain-gripped, angry dog by the time I reached the town. The town was ugly, littered with duty-free shops and rabid consumers. I tried to blend in, which was laughable. If the patroller or one of his partners spotted me, I had no way to run, and in my delirium I planned on whacking and stabbing him with my poles to get away.

Just as the sun set, I found the Ferienwohnung apartments on the outskirts and knocked on number three. The door opened and I shoved the metal tubes into the arms of a red-haired, Irish-looking maid. She did a double take, unnerved by my cantankerous face, before she shut the door.

In case the patroller was still looking for me, I hobbled through the back alleys and side lanes all the way to the bus depot. Collapsing in a chair, I put my leg up on the armrest, sustaining dirty looks from the fastidious Swiss and French folks.

seventy-six

"You have the time, mate?" I heard someone ask, and I opened my eyes.

It was Mr. Beck—Hal's enforcer, the figure from the motorcycle—his square, chiseled face bearing down at me.

"It's a little after five," I said, groggily.

He nodded and moved off to the bathroom of the bus depot.

Oh shit, I thought. Is he here to let me know that Anaïs has betrayed me? Or is it about the Schieles?

Moving my leg down from the armrest, a shrapnel of pain erupted under my kneecap. I clenched my jaw, gnashed my teeth, smothering the groaning noises coming out of me, and walked to the men's room.

The urinals were all empty. Behind me, one of the stall doors opened. Mr. Beck motioned me past, toward the next one.

Beneath the dividing panel appeared a manila envelope. I picked it up off the floor and opened it. A ticket to Los Angeles from Charles de Gaulle on Air France, and a thin stack of hundred-euro notes.

"What's this for?"

"It's time to go home, Nathan."

"Does that mean the plan has changed?"

"Yes. Once you arrive in Paris, don't go to the château; go straight to the airport."

I flipped through the stack of money. "Has something gone wrong?"

"No. But there's a fifty-fifty chance the man Bernard works for will try to terminate you."

I stared into the toilet bowl. I was so physically taxed that my adrenaline only gave a little jump and it made me feel half-dead already. "Ain't that grand," I muttered.

"Nathan," I heard him say.

"What?" My eyes on the bowl.

"Move with the crowds. Don't find yourself alone. Got it?"

"Why don't I just go to Zurich and split from there? It's a lot closer."

"No, for the next eighteen hours we need you to follow the routine."

"Why?"

"We're tailing the delivery boy right now. He left Samnaun about twenty minutes ago, headed in the direction of Bern. The prince's plane landed there this morning. We think the exchange will happen tomorrow morning. If it doesn't, we'll contact you with a new plan."

"Okay," I sighed because at any moment they could sick the police on me and possibly ruin my life. "But Hal promised to get the portraits for me if something changed. The most important one is the big canvas in the last horse stall."

"We got that covered," he said.

It felt like a lie. I was an expert now.

"Hey, is everything all right with Anaïs?" I said, cringing with trepidation. "I can't get a hold of her."

"Everything's peachy as far as we know."

Another lie.

"No, it's not," I told him. "She's not calling me back."

He paused. "We had to let Bernard and company see the body."

"What the hell," I said, outraged. "You guys were supposed to wait until I was long gone." But I was also relieved—it explained why she wouldn't be answering her phone, giving me hope that I was wrong, that she hadn't set me up like a bowling pin.

"We had to, mate. His disappearance was giving them cold feet. They thought he'd been arrested or was ratting them out."

"Isn't this worse?"

"No. We placed him in the Seine along the Left Bank. Distraught husband returns to the city and, drunk, slips and falls into the river. He's not a rat. They proceed."

"Where's Anaïs?"

"With her mother in Paris."

I punched open the door. The adrenaline was flowing now, spiked with panic. Using the throbbing in my leg to beat down the fear, I limped out of the bathroom. The bus was leaving in a few minutes.

seventy-seven

The bus moved slowly down the twisting mountain road and I wanted it to go even slower because when it was time to disembark, I'd be exposed. If they came for me, I wouldn't even be able to run, just hobble along some dark street while they chased me down.

An hour later, it was time to transfer to the train for the main leg of the trip, and I bought a bottle of ibuprofen and a phone card in the station—there might be a couple calls I'd want to make that I wouldn't want Hal to overhear. Otherwise, if I followed Mr. Beck's instructions, I would be out of the country before the shit hit the fan, I told myself, settling in my seat.

In Buchs, the train portion ended, and everyone's passports were inspected and some people's bags were gone through as we disembarked and transferred to another bus. It would take us over the Rhine into Liechtenstein. Just as I sat down in the back, I noticed two burly men hustle onto the bus at the last second. Neither of them looked at me and both sat in the first row. But I recognized the taller one as the ski guide on the tram out of Ischgl.

A deluge of anxiety jumbled my thoughts. I closed my eyes to slow my brain. At some point, I felt the bus come to a stop. I opened my eyes and realized I was breathing like a panting dog.

They exited first. I stayed on and out the window saw a police officer writing parking tickets. He'd flip the ticket pad, smooth it out, raise his pen, and gaze off for a moment as if preparing an important lecture. I wasn't sure why but I knew he was my best chance. The driver ordered me off and I hobbled onto the sidewalk. The two burly guys were milling at the depot entrance, pretending to be waiting for someone to pick them up. I made a beeline for the cop.

"Excuse me, sir," I said in German, keeping my voice conspiratorially low. "Are you the real police or do you just write tickets?" Relying on my crude German to naively pepper the question with insult, I lifted my eyebrows impatiently.

"I'm real," he said defensively.

"Well, those two men behind you. Don't look. But they tried to sell me heroin on the bus."

The officer looked at me skeptically and I gave him a wide-eyed, frightened look that was easy to pull under the circumstances.

"I thought I should tell you."

"Ya. You did the right thing."

I waited for him to turn in their direction and then hustled to the taxi stand. Pretending to adjust my pack, I glanced behind me. The two burly guys were walking toward me, and the police officer was walking toward them. When he held up his hand, stopping them, I knocked on the taxi window.

It was a big Mercedes. I pulled out a hundred-euro note so there'd be no hassle about fitting the skis in.

"Where to?" asked the driver when I closed the door.

"Feldkirch," I said, and we took off.

Although they might have been tailing me only in order to make sure I was heading back to the château as planned, I wasn't going to hang around to find out. I assumed they'd call ahead, and that someone might be waiting for me at the Liechtenstein-Austrian border and also at the train station in Feldkirch, Austria. Furthermore, my plane ticket was booked out of Charles de Gaulle and I wasn't sure if it would work from another airport. I asked the driver if he knew about the old road that "skirted" the checkpoint into Austria.

He shook his head and I explained that the road I was looking for was close to Feldkirch, close to the Austrian border. The driver brought up a map on his GPS display and pointed at various blue and white lines, roads and highways, but none of them went up a mountain.

A few kilometers from the border, parallel to Feldkirch now, he turned off the highway and drove through a series of small communities, mostly gingerbread-looking houses, separated by farmland. I decided to change out Hal's phone card with the one I'd bought so that no one would know where I was. After a few minutes, I noticed a hill rising to my right, the top half covered in snow, which reflected out from the darkness. It had to be where I'd skied with Artur Dorfmein—the arcane road into Austria up there somewhere.

It took an hour before we finally found a road that seemed right. We snaked up a mild foothill and then the road got steep. When we hit the switchbacks, I knew it was the right one. The wooden guard tower appeared above in the headlights and we seemed to slip into the 1940s. The tires began to lose traction in the deeper snow.

"I can't go any farther," the driver told me, and he stopped.

I thanked him, and having spotted a fifth of schnapps tucked between his seat and the center console, I asked him, in German slang, if I could steal a nip. I pointed at my swollen knee. "Need a little extra help tonight," I added.

I swilled down eight more pills, and the schnapps burned my chest and boosted my depraved spirits. After helping maneuver the car around, pushing the ass end sideways in the snow, I waved goodbye. The headlights streaked across the lower part of the hill and then suddenly the car was too low, too far down below me, and the hill went black as coal.

I put on my headlamp, changed into my ski boots, parka, and hat, clicked into my bindings, and set off across the hillside. If I needed to climb at any point, my skins were in the pack, but I doubted my tenuous knee would allow me to endure much more than this mild traverse.

seventy-eight

By sunrise I could see the town of Feldkirch far below. It looked like a miniature model, especially the medieval castle on the bluff. The secret road was only a hundred meters beneath me, and it wound down the hill and blended into another snow-dusted track that cut through the countryside. That track weaved onto a paved road that worked its way like a crooked creek onto a highway coming out of Feldkirch. At some point in the night, after numbing my knee several times with snow, I had crossed the border into Austria.

Clicking out of the bindings, I sat down and opened my backpack. On top was the tamper tape I'd bought in Paris with Anaïs. In my weariness at the pensione in Ischgl, I'd left the used end exposed and it was stuck on a flannel shirt. After delicately peeling away the tape, I unrolled the flannel in my lap.

The image tucked inside, now set against the crystalline air and rolling glades of snow, radiated off the paper. Egon Schiele's *Reclining Nude, Left Leg Raised*. The woman in the portrait, grasping to hold her poise while simultaneously expressing herself erotically, alone with me in the high country, was asking for my desire without sacrificing any of her dignity. Her essence pinpointed a timeless, fundamentally human moment—vulnerable and full of sensuality, asking to still be loved and respected—and it reinforced why I was risking my life to preserve her.

I sat with her for a spell. Unfurled the other three Schieles, each one a revelation. I took my time with them. When the sun got too bright, I rolled them back into my flannels and packed them away.

Then I called Artur Dorfmein.

seventy-nine

The Innsbruck station was crowded, good camouflage, while at the same time anyone looking for me would also be camouflaged. After eating breakfast, I downed one of Artur's painkillers and called Anaïs's landline from a phone booth.

The phone rang and rang. She must be in a black hole of despair over her father's death, buried away, unreachable, I thought, and I flashed on her, curled on the ground, twelve years old. I tried her cell and it went straight to voicemail. I did not mention the video; I didn't want to burden her with yet another source of anguish. Instead I left her one specific request, hung up, and headed for my train.

Mr. Beck's eighteen-hour timeline expired at noon and I was still four hours from Paris. I guessed that the Swiss scoundrel would have opened the metal tubes by now and discovered that the Schieles had been replaced with my two portraits of Anaïs. I'd sacrificed them because there was always the outside chance that the delivery boy might open the tubes before leaving the apartment, or at some point along the way to Bern, and I counted on the fact that he'd most likely just give the contents a cursory glance, or, at the very most, peek to make sure there were in fact erotic drawings in the tubes.

Even though the Swiss scoundrel would obviously check the contents once the tubes arrived in Bern, and as a result abort the exchange with the prince, I figured that Hal would at least now be able to identify him and would find another way to bust him. What I didn't know was whether or not Bernard had been arrested. Or if

Hal had gotten wind of my double cross yet and was going to arrest me too—I'd anticipated being on an airplane by now.

When I disembarked in Gare de l'Est that afternoon, I wasn't sure what to expect. Would Mr. Beck or Bernard or the Swiss guy's associates, or all of them, be looking for me?

Walking the platform, I pulled my ski cap down over my brow, eyes on the ground, and chastised myself for not abandoning the skis long ago, a glaring *come and get me*. The storage facility was in the back of the station. I checked in the skis and then called Anaïs's apartment again.

"Oui," answered Sophie.

"Is Anaïs with you?"

"No. I cannot find her."

"Are you okay?"

"No. No. They found his body in the Seine, Nathan. How can that be?"

"I have no idea."

"I don't believe you. Where are you? Bernard keeps calling me, looking for you."

Was someone there listening? If so, she would ask me to come over, lure me in. And why wasn't she at her own apartment? Regardless, I hung up.

The only rational choice was to take a taxi to the airport and get out.

eighty

Stepping on the train, I decided to trade back the new phone card with the one Hal had given me, just in case Anaïs had tried to call or text on that number. The train was packed and as I stood in a long line in the aisle, I popped in Hal's card. Instantly, a chain of texts appeared from Janet.

Where are you? . . . Please call me back . . . Are you okay?

The line started to move and with nowhere to sit I made my way into the next wagon, planning on changing the card back out once I found a seat. The phone rang. Thankfully it wasn't Hal.

"Hey, Janet."

"Is everything okay?"

"Yeah, sorry, my battery died and I had no way to charge it."

"Ah. I have good news," she said.

"That's a relief."

"I was having lunch earlier today with Michael Dolson. Do you know who he is?"

"The collector?"

"That's the understatement of the decade. He's probably the biggest in America right now. Anyway, he asked about the upcoming show and on a lark I showed him the photo you sent of the double portrait."

I stopped walking and was standing motionless in the aisle, holding my breath.

"Nathan, can you hear me?"

"Yeah, what did Dolson say?"

"He was very moved. And he wants to see the real thing. He told me it was potentially what he's been looking for."

Someone tapped me on the shoulder. I was blocking the aisle and I started moving again.

"Did you hear what I said?"

"Yeah, that's fantastic. I'm on my way to get the double portrait right now."

"Great. I called the gallery and took care of the costs, so just get it there ASAP."

"No problem. I'm on it. Thank you."

"Thank you, Nathan. And please thank your wonderful women."

eighty-one

They'd expect me to run, get out of France. Not return to the château, I reassured myself. It would be the last place I'd go. Then I changed out the phone card so that Hal couldn't track me.

Taxis didn't serve the remote train stop in Grez, so I got off in Fontainebleau and took a taxi, a mini Ford courier van, from there. On the hill overlooking the entrance gate, I had the driver pull over. From that vantage point, I could see the last half of the driveway curving to the front of the house. No cars. No movement. The corner of the house eclipsed the driveway where it forked off, went around the back, and connected with the dirt track. I ripped a hundred-euro note in two and gave the driver one half.

"Wait for me . . ."

I trotted down the incline and spied through a bullet hole in the gate. I could see the first half of the driveway now, but not beyond where it split and went around the corner of the house. No cars or people on this side of the house. I watched the big windows for a few minutes. No shadows. Nothing moving inside.

Opening the gate, I waved the taxi through; I closed the gate and gestured for him to follow me along the driveway. I passed the first stall. The double portrait, everything I aspired toward, was hidden in there.

"Wait here," I told the driver. "I'll be right back."

Before I grabbed the canvas and got the hell out, I had one more thing to do.

I followed the driveway around the back of the château onto the track. The unsteady pile of wood—the Holz Hausen—came into view. Circling to the rear of the pile, I reached the opening and looked inside. A jolt went down my legs, the shock of seeing her again when I believed I never would. Anaïs was lying on the ground, staring at the sky. She had a book with her and she was wearing headphones. I approached carefully but managed to startle her anyway. She bolted upright and screamed.

"It's okay," I said. "It's me."

She shook her head and pulled out her earbuds. "Stay away from me," she growled.

"Anaïs . . ."

"Why would Papa kill himself? Answer me that? Why would he leave me? There has to be a reason."

"He didn't leave you. He was involved with some bad people."

"No, no. The police said he committed suicide . . ."

"Anaïs. Those Schieles Bernard had were stolen. Your father and Bernard fence stolen art through a guy in Switzerland. That was the errand I had to do. Carry the Schieles across the border on skis. Something very bad is going down."

Her head was shaking but her eyes stuttered and then froze in place, as if some previous tidbit of information, something she'd heard or seen or had suspected, converged with what I was telling her. Still, it was too much for her to digest. She shook her head.

"I'm in real danger," I told her. "You might be too. You could also get arrested. But please. We have to go . . ."

"Why are you here?" she insisted.

"I came to get you. And a portrait I left in the horse stall."

"No." She swung the back of her hand at me. "No more about your work." She took in a sharp breath, held it. "You should have to choose."

"Choose what?" I said, growing anxious about time.

"Choose between me or your fucking portraits."

Fed up, I pointed toward the stalls and said, "You need to follow me to the taxi waiting for us in the drive. Now!"

As I walked around the corner of the château, I saw a sedan—BMW or Mercedes—rolling to a stop at the top of the hill above the gate. Shit. Bernard leaned out the passenger window and squinted at the drive—fortunately the taxi was too far up the drive for Bernard to see it. I eased back around the corner, hidden from him, but could still partially see the taxi driver. He was leaning against the hood of the taxi.

Turning to warn Anaïs not to follow me, I saw her standing in front of the woodpile, lagging far behind. I raised my hand. Stay put. She scoffed.

I peeked around the corner. Bernard had ducked back into the sedan. I couldn't see through the reflections in the windshield, and for the moment the sedan was not moving.

My eyes fell to the last stall and stayed riveted there.

If Michael Dolson bought the double portrait for his collection, it would change my career, doors would fly open, critics would take notice, and I'd have a chance to really excel. No longer some dreamer who'd wasted his life in pursuit of art. Everything I'd worked for as an artist was inside that stall.

Crouched, the torn ligaments in my damaged knee were throbbing. I set my jaw and debated if I would have time to open the stall, grab the canvas, hobble back to the taxi, then grab Anaïs—allowing a certain amount of time for that struggle—with enough of a head start down the dirt track before they got through the gate.

Maybe.

Once I stepped around the corner of the château, Bernard would have an opportunity to spot me. If he did, they'd come tearing down that hill. And there'd be barely enough time to grab the canvas, much less stop for Anaïs.

The taxi driver spotted me, crouched and tucked away, and wanted some sort of clue as to what the hell I was doing.

I held up my hand. Please, one minute.

I turned to Anaïs. She'd moved a few feet closer onto the edge of the track. She had one hand on her hip, as if to ask, What do you choose?

Her question, like her entire being, was a protest against everything but acting out of passion, a way of living that had helped me produce my most important work, the thing that would change my life, and I felt the double portrait pulsate behind me, warning me not to ignore it. There was no time to spare. I had to make a run for it. Now or never.

Anaïs opened her arms. What do you choose?

Don't be stupid, Nathan. The choice has been made for you. Take the canvas.

Like a falling shadow from a fast-moving cloud, the light dimmed and then came back. In that flicker of time, the scene had changed; it was as if I were the sun, piercing a haze, and whatever it was that hung over my craving for recognition began to burn away; standing in the growing beam of light, I saw Anaïs, the source of my creative virility. Regardless of the games with her mother, her manipulative family, the suspicious video, I knew that she was the embodiment of what I was really after.

Even while I waved the taxi forward, staying behind the corner of the château, I couldn't believe what I was doing. The driver took his time getting in and starting the car, before putting it in gear, and it made my decision all the more agonizing.

Something squealed. I peered around the corner. The sedan was no longer on the hill. The noise was coming from the stake that held the gate shut, lifting and grating against its metal clasps.

"Come on!" I yelled at the taxi.

He sped up.

"Get in, Anaïs! Get in!" I urged her along.

She stepped forward. I waved the taxi past me, toward her, sauntering at her own pace. The taxi pulled up alongside her.

"Open the back," she told him, suspecting I might have hidden the portraits there.

Running, one leg dragging behind, I swerved to her side of the car, grabbed her, and shoved her into the backseat. Reaching with my free hand, I dug out a clump of hundred-euro notes and dropped them on the taxi driver's lap.

"Allez!" I called over Anaïs's kicking and screaming. "You don't want those guys to catch us, I promise you!"

His mouth puckered up under his nose and he shook his head. I lunged between the seats, pulled the door handle, and rammed him out of the car. In the side mirror, I saw Bernard close the gate, a rifle in one hand, while the sedan's passenger door flung open.

In the backseat, Anaïs had stopped kicking and screaming—she was looking out the back window, watching Bernard point at us as he got into the sedan.

I jammed the taxi into gear and we skidded forward, fishtailing along the track, further behind the château, affording us a few seconds of cover.

"Where does this road go?" I yelled.

Her face hardly moved when she spoke. "To the highway on the other side of Grez."

I accelerated, wishing we had more than a mini courier van to outrun the German sedan.

"The Holz Hausen!" Anaïs hollered, pointing at the woodpile as it came parallel with my window. "Kick away the sticks! Block the road!"

Hitting the brakes, I flew out of the car, rushing in a kind of crab-walk for the woodpile behind us, and kicked, with my good leg, the base of all five sticks. Cords of wood spilled across the track, two feet high, piling up against some old chicken coops on the other side of the track. The road was choked off—for as long as it would take them to clear it away.

I heard the sedan burning up clay as I hunkered back into the taxi. I hit the gas and we climbed with a gradual curve. I glanced into the mirror again. The sedan was breaking, skidding, before it hit the wood. I heard its undercarriage bang, chunks splintering, snapping, hopefully damaging the car. Then the forest cut them off, the road had bent far enough around, and we were out of the line of fire.

eighty-two

The deep ruts in the road were threatening to bounce us into the trees. We had a little breathing room now. I eased off the pedal.

"How long till we reach the highway?" I called to Anaïs in the backseat.

"Ten minutes."

"Where is the closest airport?"

"Back through Grez."

That's no good. "What about in the other direction?"

"Orleans."

"How far?"

"An hour."

"Did you get my message about your passport?"

"Yes. I have it."

"Good."

She stared between the front seats, out the windshield, a wreck of confusion and pain, but I had to focus on the road, keep my thoughts in order.

The path curved the other way, shedding the forest, and soon we were edging along the riverbank. The setting sun had dipped below the clouds, glimmering across the water.

"Why did you come for me?" she seemed to be talking to the river. "Why?"

"What do you mean?"

Her eyes slashed at me. "Henri sent the video. He showed me."

She had believed that the video was enough to sabotage us. That I'd never come for her. And I thought of Schiele's model for *Reclining Nude, Left Leg Raised*, asking for my desire without sacrificing any of her dignity, much like what Anaïs had been asking of Henri, looking for a way to heal, longing for compassion. And I took pleasure in the notion that I would understand her, accept her, where Henri could not.

When I glanced in the rearview, she was still watching me out of the corner of her eyes. Before I could speak, a ditch threw us into the air. We landed with a crunch and suddenly there was a fork in the road.

"Left or right?" I said.

"Left takes us back toward Grez," she said, and I veered right.

The tires kicked up spindles of dust, curling skyward. I watched the spindles in the side mirror and hoped they wouldn't rise above the tree line and give us away. I felt Anaïs's lips on my cheek, warm pillows against my skin, and she whispered in my ear.

"You chose me."

My double portrait was gone.

eighty-three

It was seventy-six degrees in Los Angeles when we landed.

My phone was missing, likely lost in the tussle at the château, and I didn't want to use Anaïs's, so I found a pay phone in the terminal. I called Janet and told her I was back in L.A. with my girlfriend, that her father just passed away, and we needed some privacy, but I didn't mention the drawings. Could we crash at her pad for a few days?

"No problem. I'll stay at Gary's," she said, and she asked about the double portrait.

"It's on the way," I lied. "Thanks for giving us some space."

An hour later, I picked up a key from the gallery receptionist, and Anaïs and I walked next door to Janet's apartment building. Art Deco moldings, an apple-red fire escape zigzagging from the fourth floor to the second. Understandably, Anaïs was devastated; she'd wavered between crying and staring listlessly into space during the entire flight, and now the dark shadows under her eyes made her look ten years older and sickly. I took her hand, helping her up to the second floor, which was arduous with my bum knee. Once we were inside, she drank three tall cups of water, found the bed, and crawled under the covers. I sat beside her and rubbed her back. What else was there to do?

We stayed inside the following day and I mulled over our options—How would we make money? Where would we live?—while the cacophony of questions about Sophie and Bernard, the mess we'd left behind, tried to pry their way in. Was I a fugitive? It was hard to know. Most importantly, I was home and with Anaïs. We could make more great paintings. We could make a life together.

That night, she insisted on calling her mother. Although the FBI and a group of criminals were looking for us—at least for me—because they wanted those Schieles, I understood the necessity to make sure her mother was okay.

I walked Anaïs down the street to a pay phone, and standing beside her with my hand on the cradle hook, listened, ready to hang up if I sensed she was about to give away our location. After hearing that Sophie was not in jail or feeling threatened, and after Anaïs convinced her that she was somewhere safe with me, I interrupted.

"Tell her you'll call back in a week or so," I said quietly.

Anaïs shook her head, whispering, "Maman is all alone. She said Bernard is gone."

I put my hand on her shoulder. "Your mom's smart and tough. She'll pull through. Now say good-bye."

She told Sophie she'd call back soon and reluctantly hung up.

The next morning, I persuaded her to walk to the beach and go for a dip in the ocean. She refused to wear a bra or underwear. Nearby sunbathers and a couple joggers made a stink, forcing the lifeguards, clearly against their will, to ask her to get out of the ocean and put her clothes back on. She stomped away, toward the apartment, naked. As I tried to catch up with her, it was apparent that the saltwater, washing around my knee, had freed up the ligament and muscle, and it was no longer excessively painful.

I poached two eggs and fried some bacon and she ate in front of the TV. It would be a long wait, I knew, before she would climb out of her mourning.

On the fourth day, after I returned from the market, Janet called.

"The show's in two days," she said. "Where is the double portrait?"

"It'll be here by tomorrow," I assured her.

"It better be, Nathan. I used the photo you sent for the catalogue and the promotions."

"No problem, it'll be here," I said. "Hey, do you have any paper and pencils lying around? I'd like to work."

"You have to ask Cindy," she said. "Her office is behind reception. She might have something back there."

When I returned with a pile of paper and a box of good charcoal pencils, Anaïs was in the bath. I started drawing her. She shook her head and turned away with disdain.

"Anaïs," I appealed. "We have to do something. We can't just sit here and be depressed. We're almost out of money. Janet's going to kick us out soon. Our only chance is to make something for the show."

She remained despondent but I kept working because it seemed like our only chance of survival. I made two fairly good drawings and went to Blick to get some watercolors. After paying, we had a hundred and thirty-five dollars left.

I worked all night and Anaïs just watched TV and smoked cigarettes. With her vitality and spirit in shambles, she was a different person, and it broke my heart. I feared we'd soon reach the end of our capacity to thrive. With nothing left to connect us, to keep the passion going, we were dead.

eighty-four

Anaïs was on the couch, watching TV, and I was trying to spruce up the drawings when Janet opened the door. Her face was strained.

"Sorry to intrude, but we're putting up the final pieces now. I need the double portrait."

"The shipping company says it's missing," I told her, glancing at Anaïs to see if she was listening. Her eyes were glued to a soap opera. I lifted up the drawings I'd been working on. "But I have these for you."

Janet walked past the couch, glancing at Anaïs, who ignored her, and I handed her the two new pieces, hoping she'd just take them out of necessity. She laid them on the bench by the window.

"These look rushed. They're nowhere close to the double." She turned around and faced me. "I'm going to have to use John Selters's drawings in place of yours."

"Wait, I can polish these out right now," I insisted.

"It's too late. You blew it."

"The shipping people screwed me."

"I called the gallery in Paris, Nathan. You never gave them anything to ship."

"I had to use a different place. Long story."

"I'm sure it is." Her heels clacked as she moved to the door. "Please be out by tomorrow," she said, glancing at Anaïs, catatonic on the couch. "I'm sorry for your loss."

eighty-five

In the morning, I headed for the boardwalk with some paper and pencils. Staying in my work was the only way to contend with the terrible disappointment and the bleakness I felt.

The morning fog was lifting and as I got closer to the kiosks, the thinning veil revealed a carnival of disco-dancing roller skaters, scrappy artists selling their wares, beefy body builders, surfers, skateboarders, and homeless encampments, interwoven with the hordes that came to look at it all.

The young homeless kids, huddled in groups as large as twenty or thirty on the grassy knoll in the middle of the hubbub, were the most interesting. A lot of them had pit bulls or Rottweilers, and musical instruments, and a few had high-end backpacks. They all seemed inured to a daily routine of begging, hanging out, scoring drugs, and partying late into the night.

I might be joining their ranks soon, I told myself, as I drew a teenage boy, dirt smudges on his face, staring into his iPhone. The girl sitting beside him, covered by an oversized hoodie, had been tapping his shoulder trying to get his attention. Fed up now, she shoved him with both hands and stood, lifting her skateboard with her.

"This is bullshit," she sniped. "All you do is play that crap all day. I'm going to skate the pool . . ."

Ripping back the hood, she pivoted and was marching right at me. She had grey-green eyes and a mane of strawberry blonde hair that fell past her cut-off jeans. Sweeping by me, her hair was like a cape, a strawberry sea, with the palm fronds bursting out above her in the sky.

I got to my feet and followed her toward the skate park. Capturing her airing out of a pool with that crazy hair would be a very contemporary, romantic image. I watched her bum a cigarette off a black kid and then she leaned against the skate park railing and shot the shit with the other onlookers. After ten minutes, I realized she didn't actually skateboard; she just carried one around as an accessory.

On my way back to the apartment, someone called out my name.

"Long time no dance," Hal said, rolling up on a beach-cruiser bicycle, a fresh sunburn splotching his pale skin.

"I was wondering when I'd hear from you."

"Things ain't going so well, huh?" he said.

"Nope."

"You kinda screwed me."

"How's that? By putting my life on the line for you?"

"You didn't help yourself with your little stunt."

I shrugged indignantly.

"You know," he said, "we almost moved in on the Swiss dude. Only at the last second did we realize he didn't have the Schieles. Could've been a real embarrassment for us."

"But now you know who he is," I asserted.

"Yep. That's the good part. Would've saved a lot of time and resources to bust him then and there."

I nodded and he nodded.

"What about Bernard?" I said.

"No Schieles, no smoking gun. But the fellas he works with are after his scalp." He laughed. "That's far worse than us."

"Shit." I hadn't thought that part through.

"Where are they, Nathan?"

I pulled one of the pencils from my pocket and tore off a corner from one of my drawing sheets, writing down *Artur Dorfmein.*

"He lives in Feldkirch, Austria," I said. "Drives the train between Feldkirch and Innsbruck. Easy to find."

Hal stuffed the piece of paper in his windbreaker.

"My colleagues were convinced that you'd sold them," he said. "But I knew you just wanted to protect the Schieles. *Old Nathan has tucked them away somewhere safe,* I told them. And I was right."

"Yep, Hal, you were right."

He rolled onto the balls of his feet, mouth and cheeks forming a glowering expression.

I stepped across the boardwalk.

eighty-six

Anaïs was asleep on the couch. A pall of dejection infused the apartment, deepened by the fact that we were about to get booted. With her thoroughly down and out, it was my role to keep fighting. I knew what I was capable of and I needed to go make it happen. Wolfing down a meager sandwich, I went back out to look for a spark of inspiration.

A swim, like I used to do at the château, would do me good. The ocean was cold but the air was warm. I swam under the rolling surf and thought about my grandfather, what he might say to me right now. *Like all things it's part of a cycle; stay with it and you'll come around.* A big swell lifted me and when it passed the wide fan of ocean stretched all the way under the horizon line into some twilight beyond, and I thought about taking Anaïs up to Portland for the holidays; we'd stay with my parents; maybe Alice would be in town with her family. But in the time it took to bodysurf a wave and wash onto the beach, the idea had crumbled.

I walked to the Santa Monica Pier and watched the Ferris wheel twirling in the sky. I lay facedown in the sand and replayed that moment at the château when I'd turned my back on the double portrait, my golden ticket, for the promise of making more art with Anaïs, making a life with her, flourishing in love. Now it all felt like the sand falling through my fingers.

By five, the sun was about to set. It was low tide and I walked in the wet sand, meandering back to Venice.

Around six o'clock, I crossed the boardwalk onto where Venice Boulevard began its stretch from the Pacific toward the city. The gallery and apartment were just up the street. Throngs of people were stepping out of Ubers and expensive cars, well dressed, crowding into the gallery. I couldn't bear to go inside and see what I should have been a part of. I felt like an interloper crashing someone else's show. I turned around and took the back alley to the apartment building, entering from there.

The TV was off. It was quiet. Moving into the bedroom, I saw that the bed was made. Her scent, distilled to a tobacco stench, hung in the air. She was gone. Maybe I could catch her at LAX. Had her mother wired money? Somehow arranged a plane ticket back to France?

The room felt clogged, stale, dusty. I needed to sit down. The floor seemed best. Then I lay all the way down, resting my cheek on the checkered linoleum, and I thought of Wes ending the pain.

The front door creaked open. It couldn't be Anaïs, and I hoped that whoever it was would go away. I heard the person pad into the bedroom.

"Nathan, are you all right?"

Janet appeared beside me, crouching.

"Just resting," I mumbled.

"Well get up." She shook me. "Do you have a nice shirt at least?"

"No."

She pulled a clean shirt off a hanger in the closet, presumably one of Gary's. "Put this on," she said.

"No."

"But you can't look like that."

"Who gives a shit how I look?"

"Michael Dolson does."

"Let me rest. Please."

"Get off the floor."

I sighed. "Why?"

"Because the double portrait is downstairs. The note said it's called *French Girl with Mother.*"

I studied her face to make sure I wasn't having a weird dream. Her features were in shadow and I squinted.

Janet continued talking. "It arrived with three other drawings of Anaïs, very erotic, clearly your homage to Schiele, about an hour ago. The note was from someone named Hal."

I took a deep breath. Blinked a few times.

"Anyway, Dolson is head over heels about the double portrait. I came up here to get you but you were gone, so Anaïs came down."

It must be a dream.

eighty-seven

I pushed through the crowd, head down, and when I finally looked up it was really there. Sophie and Anaïs, spider and prey, mother and daughter, that magnetic confrontation.

Someone was talking to me, and an orgy of bodies oscillated around me, gawking, asking questions. I touched one person's face to make sure it was real. When I looked at the painting again, I saw myself in the two figures, my torment and longing, darkness and light, wanting love while fighting for recognition. Life, like art, is ultimately a struggle with yourself, I thought. Something drew me to the stairs on the other side of the room.

Anaïs was sitting on the landing, bent low so she could peer just under the archway and view the double portrait from a distance. How long has she been studying it? I wondered. Her face was angular, spiteful, but the eyes were practically hanging, bagged. Would she suddenly bound down the stairs and rip the canvas off the wall and try to destroy it? I crossed the room, climbed the stairs, stopping on the last step before the landing, and waited for her to acknowledge me.

"Is there anything else I should know?" she said.

"I would do it all over again."

Her eyes dropped onto me, a whiff of loathing behind shattered glass. The corners of her mouth were pulled down.

"Even after what has happened to us, would you still choose me?"

Her head tilted to one side, letting the ceiling lights enhance her blackened eyes.

I eased onto the landing, kneeled and kissed her, my answer.

She bit my lip hard. "No, you wouldn't," she retorted.

I pulled away but she wrapped her arms and legs around me, an anchor. Her mouth nuzzled my ear and her grip tightened.

"I should hate you," she hissed in my ear.

Tasting blood on my tongue, I waited. Nothing more, the rest was implied, her warm breath in my ear.

I could feel a mass of eyes from below, turning and setting on us. Their voices dimmed, decibel by decibel. The last sounds were dying out when she gestured toward the double portrait.

"You should put our names on it."

I came nose to nose with her. Searched her expression to make sure I'd heard her correctly. No trace of apprehension in those eyes, impassioned now. The first muse in history to insist on coauthorship with not only the artist but also a fellow muse, her mother.

She had a point. We'd all made that painting together.

Her finger wiped a drop of blood off my lip, held it up like ink on the tip of a fountain pen. "Woods . . . Blanchon . . . Blanchon . . ." she said, drawing our names in the air. One side of her mouth curved into a funny grin and I knew what our next great painting would be.